DATE DUE

TILL THE FAT
LADY SINGS

TILL THE FAT LADY SINGS

ALISA KWITNEY

Aaron Asher Books
HarperCollins*Publishers*

HarperCollins books may be purchased for educational, business, or sales promotional use. For information, please write: Special Markets Department, HarperCollins Publishers, Inc., 10 East 53rd Street, New York, NY 10022.

FIRST EDITION

Designed by Claudyne Bianco

Library of Congress Cataloging-in-Publication Data
Kwitney, Alisa, 1964–
    Till the fat lady sings/Alisa Kwitney.—1st ed.
        p.   cm.
    ISBN 0-06-019021-3 (cloth)
    I. Title.
    PS3561.W53T55   1992
    813'.54—dc20   92-52552

92 93 94 95 96 ❖/HC 10 9 8 7 6 5 4 3 2 1

For my mother, Ziva

TILL THE FAT
LADY SINGS

FOOD FOR THOUGHT

~~

Do you know what you had for breakfast today? How about yesterday? Can you remember what you ate for dinner last week?

Manya could. It was not that Manya's memory was necessarily better than average—although Manya *was* only eighteen, and her brain cells had never been damaged by large amounts of alcohol or chemicals. The reason Manya could remember what she'd had for breakfast the day before (two pieces of toast with low-cal margarine and black coffee) and even the day before that (six hot cross buns and a pint of chocolate milk) was that she wrote down everything she ate in a little blue clothbound diary.

Do you know how many calories a hot cross bun contains? Can you guess how long it takes your body to digest a hot cross bun? How about a hot dog smothered in cheese, or an artichoke? Manya knew.

The other people in Manya's dormitory did not know about her secret expertise. To them, she was a bland and rather uninteresting addition to a hall where one girl kept her shades drawn day and night and played tapes of whale sounds, one boy claimed to have mastered the art of out-of-body meditation, and another boy wore black robes whenever he fed a mouse to his pet anaconda. Manya possessed no overtly remarkable talents or quirks, espoused no passionate beliefs, and did not come from a foreign country. She was a vague and subtle watercolor on a canvas splashed with vivid oils. As far as her living companions were concerned, she barely existed.

Do not judge these people prematurely. The girl who kept her shades drawn had been offered scholarships to three Ivy League colleges and had chosen Columbia despite a fierce hatred of cities, and the boy with the anaconda was struggling with his sexual identity and planning to study comparative religion. College, after all, is a sort of theater where young people come to improvise themselves. Ideas such as existentialism, deconstructionism, Marxism, and feminism are there to be tried on for effect; some may prove so comfortable that they are never fully discarded, while others, as outdated as hoop skirts, prevent the wearer from entering the doors to the future and must be cut down to size or cast off completely.

As for Manya, she saw at a glance that the costumes that would fit her did not suit her, and the ones that suited did not fit. Not that she minded all that much; she preferred research to improvisation. In college as in life, however, both skills are necessary.

THE FIRST COURSE

~

"Now, I know that all of you are extremely anxious for me to explain what we'll be doing in this course so that you can either scurry off and purchase your books or else drop this class from your schedule." Professor Larsdatter paused. "But I personally do not hold with the practice of going over my entire syllabus as if I were trying to sell you all a vacuum cleaner."

Professor Larsdatter was a slender, elegant woman in her mid to late thirties. Her hair was pulled back in a bun and held there by two dangerously long and sharp Victorian tortoiseshell combs. She wore tortoiseshell glasses and very dark, very red lipstick. Her class, A Feminist Reading of Victorian Novels, was relegated to a basement room in the science building, a room that was difficult to find among the winding subterranean corridors and cavernous laboratories. Nevertheless, ten undergraduate English majors, all female, and two "qualified freshmen" had managed to traverse this maze.

"What I am willing to say," she continued, "is that we will be studying a number of Victorian texts, the names of which you can find on the sheet of paper I just handed out. We will be reading them from a feminist perspective, and when I say 'feminist' I mean as pertains to literary theory, not as pertains to your individual convictions or lack thereof. From this perspective, we will address the subtext of these works. We will examine how the Victorian mistrust of women's appetites, like their view of progress, flows through the hidden caverns of our society. We will also challenge the notion that women should have smaller appetites than men—both as regards food and as regards sex." Professor Larsdatter gave the word "sex" a particularly sharp inflection, and then drew a deep breath, as if irritated at having to state something so obvious. "Any questions?"

Manya, who had been scribbling all this down in her notebook, raised her hand.

"Yes?"

"But women today aren't expected to have less sexual desire than men, are they?" Manya's reticence did not extend to the classroom. The formal structure of a class, in which relationships were clearly defined and subject matter determined within given boundaries, freed her of inhibition. Moreover, she believed in asking questions in class. She did not assume that her lack of understanding stemmed from congenital stupidity, nor did she assume that her questions would be resolved in due course. An unasked question, she felt, was seldom answered.

Professor Larsdatter regarded her coolly over the rims of her lowered spectacles. "There is an argument, I suppose, that now that the sexual revolution has come and gone, women are men's equals. More or less." She paced slowly as she spoke, her high heels clicking on the tiled floor. "But the aim of this course is to illustrate, through source material, how women persist in imaging themselves as objects rather than agents of desire. To disagree with this premise, one should be well acquainted with the distinction between what the culture claims it says and what it really says. Any other questions? No? Then if I may continue ..."

Professor Larsdatter might as well have plucked one of her sharp combs from its bed of hair and inserted it into Manya's chest. Manya, who had not realized that her question would drop like a gauntlet at Larsdatter's feet, was shocked to find she had been so summarily dispatched. In high school, her comments had always received a considered and almost gratified response from her teachers. Obviously, there were rules involved here, like the rules of swordplay—rules which refined the battle of wits, making it infinitely more dangerous.

A verbal misstep could prove treacherous, Manya saw, for she could lose more than the argument; she could lose face as well. Manya felt the first inklings of intellectual self-doubt. And this was not just some compulsory course, this was subject matter dear to her heart. Wounded but not yet defeated, Manya resolved to plunge ahead, to attack the vague fleshy monster of her ignorance with Professor Larsdatter's weapons. Victorian texts, literary theory, feminist theory—whatever was required, she would do.

But first, after the introductory lecture was over, she promised herself a large order of french fries and a box of Pop-Tarts.

MANYA

~~

Manya Miriam Mittelman, born weighing six pounds and five ounces in Maplewood, New Jersey, just as women's lib was becoming a household word, now carried one hundred and thirty-five pounds on her five-foot-two-inch frame. Which is to say, according to mainstream standards of female beauty, specifically the standards of Western civilization in the late twentieth century, that Manya was considered plump. Renoir would have adored her; Rubens might have argued that her breasts were too big. In Egypt, Haiti, and other places where ample feminine pulchritude is still prized, Manya would be worth her weight in ... well, simply worth her weight.

But in the subculture of Columbia University on Manhattan's Upper Upper West Side, where shaved heads and nose rings enjoyed a certain popularity, avoirdupois was definitely not admired. Manya passed through the first weeks of her freshman year as an all but anonymous blur to her classmates, despite participating in a "welcome to college" barbecue and sitting in a circle with the other students on her hall for a two-hour discussion of what each person had done over the summer. Had she been on a campus in the middle of a flat expanse of wheat or in the kind of college town where every business, from drugstore to pizza parlor, depends upon the trade of students, Manya would have made a few friends. On a lifeboat adrift in an uncharted ocean, even loners will tend to socialize. But Columbia is not a lifeboat; it is more like a tributary, pouring students like hapless salmon into the serious depths of the waters that surround it.

Manya settled into her solitude. She was not so much content with her lot as resigned to it; she viewed herself as a four-year hostage to higher education. Manya's companions were the heroines of the books and plays she read: Jane Austen's headstrong Emma, Bernard Shaw's wily Ann Whitefield, Oscar Wilde's opinionated Gwendolen. Manya preferred her heroines feminine, determined, and witty. Their battles may have taken place in English drawing rooms, but they were generals nonetheless. They may have disdained the appearance of effort, but they were never without goals. They were not the sort of women who went to fraternity parties and misplaced their underwear in somebody else's bed. They married but did not mate. The earthiest thing they did was putter about in their gardens.

Manya felt that beauty was not something to be achieved.

Her heroines did not strive after beauty; if they were lovely, it was because loveliness had simply been granted them, like a papal dispensation. Because she knew she was not lovely, Manya did not sabotage her looks in the way that many women, at the peak of physical beauty and health, tend to do upon entering college, refusing to bathe or wear deodorant, dying blonde hair black and dressing in shrouds.

Manya was always scrupulously clean; she fairly hummed with fresh-scrubbed, talcum-powdered, vigorously brushed care. She had the kind of face humans have spent centuries breeding into lapdogs: wide-eyed, full-cheeked, with a smoothly rounded forehead partially concealed by a tousle of finely curling brown hair. Her unease in social situations manifested itself as a kind of hesitant, earnest awkwardness. Her wardrobe consisted mainly of hugely oversized men's jackets and full peasant skirts beaten soft by frequent washings, skirts so delectably worn that their original colors—red, purple, blue, yellow—were faded to the gentle glow of rose, lavender, violet, and gold that you find on the inside of certain seashells. Her one piece of jewelry was a small Victorian mourning ring.

All in all, Manya looked like a budding matron, and people tended to treat her accordingly.

She had not always been plain. She had been a startlingly lovely child, a shy little girl with a head of blonde curls, slender as a gazelle. She was one of those children whom adults find well mannered and other children find unbearably boring. Her mother, Sophie, tried to comfort her by feeding her chocolate bars, sugared cereals, cheese straws—anything and everything which other children were denied. If little Manya desired plastic fruits with strawberry-flavored sugar inside, then she could have them, as many as she liked, and as often. By the age of twelve, Manya was no longer blonde and no longer slender. Suddenly Sophie reprimanded her for eating, just as Manya's hormones were giving her an appetite. Manya entered adolescence on a cloud of resentment, and the cloud had a faint flavor of strawberry sugar and cheese straws.

"Leave me alone," Manya said to her mother, defiantly unwrapping the wax paper from a cream puff. "You'd think it was drugs."

"You're going to be fat if you're not careful," Sophie warned.

"If I am, it's your fault. You haven't been a consistent mother."

"But you're the one who will suffer, Manya. Look at it this way; if you wind up battling your weight like I do, that won't harm me. It'll make *your* life miserable."

What good did it do for Sophie to warn her daughter about the rest of her life? Adolescence is a dangerous time because suddenly the child is an adult, but without a history of adult experience. For all that childhood is meant to prepare us for life, it would be hard to say that human teenagers are better off than baby snakes, who wriggle away from their mothers' bodies moments after birth, fully formed and equipped with all the instincts they need to get by in the world.

"It's my life, and I'll be miserable if I want to," said Manya, and ate her cream puff.

BEING MISERABLE

~

Columbia University in the afternoon. Its heavy iron gates mark a small territory of neatly roped-off lawns, evenly pruned rows of trees, and a section of less than cerulean sky. It is not so much a campus as it is an illusion of a campus, for Columbia's buildings and students spill over into city streets and the denizens of city streets spill over into Columbia. Between the hours of 2:00 and 4:00 p.m. pigeons can be seen on the lawns foraging for food, debating pigeon politics, and attempting to negotiate a mating. Most students can be found similarly occupied, or else sprawled on the large, smooth, broad stairs which lead to Low Library, studying anything and everything that crosses their path, but not their books.

Manya was not among them. She was a bird of a different feather, and did not flock together with the aggressively social pigeons and students. Every day at four o'clock, when a burst of sparrows made a sudden fuss of wings and whistles near a white stone bench, Manya greeted them with the crumbs of English tea biscuits.

On this particular Friday, because it was unseasonably cold for early October, the sky seemed crisp and sharply drawn against the branches of the trees. Someone had attached a small hand-lettered poster to the trunk of one tree: HUGE CAMPUS RALLY, it read, ON DECEMBER 21, ORGANIZED BY THE DOOMSDAY COALITION. Was it a joke? Manya's mind wandered. Her bottom was growing numb through the thin cotton of her skirt, but she intended to sit until the birds descended. She was feeling intellectually inferior, she had just gained three more pounds, and Friday was always a precursor to a lonely trio of nights. As Manya sat, three of her textbooks unopened beside her on the bench, she saw a young woman laughing a little ways away, her face upturned to a young man.

"Take that back," the young woman said. Her skull, clearly revealed by her short slick helmet of platinum hair, was small and appeared unusually fragile. Her pale, pale face emerged from the high collar of a threadbare black velvet jacket which left her long, slender forearms bare. She was perversely beautiful, with a vampiric innocence about her.

"Why should I? You love to be mistreated. It makes you feel that you have a reason to be depressed." The young man was less spectacular, but cast from a similar mold. His hair stood out in a whitish stubble around his head, but a darker shadow around his chin revealed that this color was achieved through artifice. His coat was also black, a long raincoat which slapped against his knees in a sudden gust of wind.

"I have a reason to be depressed. Everyone has. Happiness passes. Everything ends in death. All things lead to decay." The young woman's voice was childlike in its nasal flatness.

"What course did you get that from? Angst 101? Really, Ophelia, you're too much."

"Piss off, then," said Ophelia, with surprising conviction.

"All right. I'll see you later?" The young man waved carelessly.

Ophelia turned to Manya, who sat some ten feet away. "You. I don't like being watched."

Manya stared in shock. She had forgotten that she was not as invisible as she felt.

Ophelia moved closer, and Manya saw that her face was contorted with fury. She was also crying.

"Am I entertaining you?"

"I'm sorry," Manya said. Her knees shook. She had poor shock absorbers for anger, and Ophelia's challenge was like a direct blow.

"You're afflicted with melancholia, aren't you?" Ophelia's whole manner changed abruptly, as if she were one of Dracula's victims, not fully a vampire herself yet, and Manya's startled fear had awakened some dormant strain of humanity still coursing through her blood. Sitting down beside Manya on the bench, she shivered quietly. Her legs were bare under a short black skirt. On her feet, she wore scuffed sneakers.

Ophelia's neurasthenic beauty, the elegance of her brooding frown, the intangible charm she exuded as she examined her toe through a hole in her sneaker, all conspired to fill Manya with a feeling of dejection. Not knowing what else to do, she stood up, gently gathering her books and holding them to her chest. She moved slowly, so as to give no offense.

"Where are we going?" asked Ophelia brightly, immediately getting up as well.

"I was going to get some chocolate," said Manya, as another person might have said, "I was going to get high." Ophelia's mercurial switches of mood threw her off balance, and she did not have time to think of a less revealing response.

"I'll go with you. You emit an aura of wistful resignation which I find oddly comforting."

Manya did not want this vampire girl trailing after her, feeding off her sadness and gaining a few hours' respite before sundown. Manya's depression, founded on feelings of self-hatred and loneliness, fortified by a sense of hopelessness and the conviction that no one out there really cared for her, was by now becoming an entire metropolis of negative emotions.

Busloads of old griefs were arriving and unloading their cargo; trains of hurt and lonely thoughts were chugging slowly through her brain. She wanted to be alone, to try and manage this teeming inner city. Tears, welling up behind her eyes, threatened to rain down upon the whole mess, and Manya knew she had to act fast.

"Please," she said, turning to Ophelia, "I really just want to be alone."

"You are alone. I'm alone. That's the way we're born, and that's the way we die."

"But before you die I'm sure you have at least three parties to go to tonight. I'm going to be sitting in my room with a book. Oh, listen, what's the use? I've got to go."

Ophelia looked at Manya with admiration. "We can be friends," she said. "I feel it in my bones. I do have parties to go to and men fawning over me and all that, but I haven't any female intimates. You would be the perfect candidate. I wouldn't threaten you or make you feel competitive because, honestly speaking, I'm way out of your league, and I have the strongest sense that you would never bore me, because you have a sort of ruthless honesty about you."

Oddly, Manya was flattered by this. Ophelia carried herself like one of Manya's heroines, and it was almost thrilling to be deemed a fitting companion by this exotic creature. But it was also frightening, and there was something that exerted a stronger pull on Manya than Ophelia did. Raisin-studded rugelach to stem the flood of tears! Chocolate-peanut-butter ice cream to cram into the empty hole of a Friday night! Egg rolls, onion rings, anything and everything, instant pleasure, pleasure to be expected and attained.

"Another time," said Manya, and stumbled off, balancing her books awkwardly on her stomach.

PROFESSOR LARSDATTER

~

Emilia Larsdatter was not a happy woman. She could have been, if not happy, then at least self-satisfied, had she only been able to believe herself what she told her friends: that the only reason her academic star had failed to rise was prejudice.

The truth was, Emilia was unoriginal. Her ideas had been espoused more dramatically, more eloquently, and with greater charm by several prominent French feminist thinkers.

Professional jealousy was not the only reason Emilia hated the French. She despised their trim figures, fashionably slender despite meals of exquisite delicacy and subtle flavor, while she had to eat packets of diet food from a company called Slim Pickin's.

When Emilia had first left Ohio to enter Columbia's graduate English program, she had been plumper than Manya. Then she'd met a man. As her pride had prevented her from embarking on a love affair so long as she was overweight, Emilia had assigned herself the task of starving one appetite in order to feed another. Though the Slim Pickin's people promised to teach their clients how to maintain their target weight while eating regular foods, Emilia persisted in subscribing to their prepackaged plan for Mature Woman Maintenance: grayish packets of powdered soup and salad dressing, red or brown frozen dinners, tiny plastic bags of pasta or rice, and thin, dry, crumbly versions of bread and cake. In this way, she avoided the worry and bother of shopping, cooking, and counting calories.

Emilia, plump? Emilia, from Ohio? Yes and yes. Born in 1954 to an Oberlin English professor named Richard Larson and his homemaker wife Lillian, Emilia had grown up as plain Emily Larson, plump and bespectacled and bookish. The late sixties and early seventies had all but passed her by. While others marched, burned their bras, smoked fat joints, and made love under the flat Ohio sky, Emilia trudged to classes and home again, to read Virginia Woolf while her mother watched television and her father graded papers. Oberlin had been a tempting place indeed when she was a student there, full of music and pot and revolution, but Emilia might as well have been in a nunnery. At a time when college as theater was at its all-time peak, when people improvised themselves more dramatically and enthusiastically than ever before or since, Emilia discovered that it is nearly impossible to reinvent yourself when your stage is the town where you were born and raised and your father is your director.

Professional jealousy was not the only reason Emilia hated her father. The esteemed Professor Larson, with his grimly amused smile and patronizing words of encouragement, tended to treat his students as beloved offspring and his only child as a nonpaying boarder in his house. Later, when she changed her name legally to Larsdatter—the Norwegian spelling of Larsdaughter—her father wrote, telling her, "As you have disowned me, so am I disowning you." "Good," she'd written back. "You wouldn't have cared if I'd changed my name by getting married, you hypocrite."

Now, grading papers of her own, Emilia glanced at the name in the top right-hand corner: Manya Miriam Mittelman. The chubby Jewish girl, thought Emilia, and then chastised herself. She did not like Manya, poor earnest Manya, because Manya reminded her of herself, her real self: layers of fat and self-loathing, carefully concealed under the fashionable tortoiseshell glasses, the red, red lipstick and sharp retorts. It was nine o'clock on a Friday night, and Emilia Larsdatter was grading papers in her small Upper West Side apartment, lonely and miserable. She knew in her heart that Manya, wherever she was, probably felt the same way, and pity mingled with loathing moved in her breast.

OPHELIA

~

Ernest Hébert (1817–1908) once painted a picture of Shakespeare's Ophelia which Emilia Larsdatter could have analyzed for hours. In it, the darkly brooding eyes seem to burn with unhallowed passion, reproaching the viewer with their madness. The drooping flowers which cascade from the model's waving blonde hair open with unrestrained sexuality, dying blossoms caught in the web of Ophelia's frustrated father-love.

It was this picture which prompted Jane Saunders, then fifteen, to change her name to Ophelia. For years Jane affected streaming uncombed hair and loose medieval gowns. Once, she even tried to drown herself in the bath, but then gave in to the languor of floating in her sodden silks, lost in the fantasy that she was a reptile, able to shed her skin and stare the world down with lidless eyes. But she was only a human teenager, and the hormones which spread like flash fire through her veins lit the fuse of her depression. So it happens with many formerly happy children. Adolescence is one of the peak times for suicide. Was it a chemical imbalance which made Ophelia, née Jane, so horribly riddled with angst and bleak despair?

Her mother was a psychologist, her father a psychiatrist. They were not bad parents, or at least, not neglectful, or abusive, or unkind. They gave their daughter love and understanding, and when this proved insufficient, they gave her lithium and antidepressants.

Ophelia, like a tragic heroine, refused to be saved for very long. By turns she was anorexic, suicidal, promiscuous, and addicted to cocaine. At times she would rally, long enough to graduate high school in a brief flurry of brilliant grades and graceful smiles, and then she would sink again. By the age of nineteen, she had already spent time under observation at Payne Whitney. The doctors there found her literate and amusing but were alarmed at the disruption she caused among the other patients, who tended to fall in love with her.

Friday night, twelve o'clock. Dr. and Dr. Saunders, do you know where your child is? Ophelia was in the bed of the young man with the white crew cut, sitting astride his chest, which was bare, drawing a skull and crossbones on his sternum with a black eye pencil. She was a good artist, very good. She drew skeletal women with streaming blonde hair and burning, brooding eyes, and obese women, fecund and fertile, their heads bent in sorrow. Her art professor thought she was the most talented student he had seen in thirteen years.

"You don't love me, do you?" asked Ophelia, finishing her picture.

"I'm incapable of love," the young man replied. His name was Arthur, and he was lying, but only a little.

"Good," said Ophelia. "I don't want anyone to love me."

"I want to fuck you," said Arthur.

"I don't want that, either," said Ophelia, but was rolled onto her back anyway, and so acquiesced.

ZAFTIGUE

~

On Saturday morning, while her hallmates slept in strange beds, or slept with strangers in their own beds, battling hangovers or still mildly drugged, Manya showered and got ready for work. The showers were deserted but smelled unpleasantly of urine, beer, and vomit; not Manya's ritual offering, but the careless unplanned vomit of drunken visitors.

Hot water, soap, and solitude. Manya was almost happy. She lifted her heavy breasts and gently let them fall, ran the soap bar over the curves of her hips, where the spidery pale tracings of stretch marks bore silent testimony to a too-rapid weight gain. Poor unloved, untouched flesh! Manya's body hair was sparse and downy, and she was proud of this. She barely needed to shave her legs or under her arms. She touched herself tentatively between her thighs, a timid greeting, and then poured a capful of green apple shampoo onto her palm. Manya was a morning person, one of those creatures whose metabolism wakes easily and fully. Her brain, which cupped sluggish and morose thoughts at night, held a full portion of hopefulness at the start of every day. Ruled by the body, as are we all, Manya mistakenly believed that her morning optimism was philosophical rather than biological. She never needed breakfast. She needed touching, but as Emilia Larsdatter would say, was too fearful of men to feel comfortable as an *agent* of desire. She was waiting for a lover to recognize her, to transform her into an *object* of desire. Sometimes it is the flesh that is willing and the spirit that is weak.

On weekends, Manya worked at a small clothes boutique on Columbus Avenue called Zaftigue. This name was derived from the Yiddish word *zaftig,* which means a little more voluptuous than voluptuous. Manya had wandered into the shop and wound up spending almost the entire day there as Boris, the shop's owner, regaled her with the tale of his last three love affairs, complained of the ache in his left elbow, and admitted to feelings of guilt over his decision to remain open for business over the Jewish holidays. Then he offered her a job.

There was no place where Manya felt more comfortable than at Zaftigue, where plaster statues of the Venus de Milo and other fleshy beauties of the past stood armless and expressionless and unclothed in the window. Inside, there were richly colored loose tunics and harem pants, draped A-line dresses, overalls with dropped waists or no waists, and even Merry Widow corsets and slinky nightgowns. In deference to the sensibilities of the boutique's clientele, there was only one slender mannequin, a 1940s relic with clunky black shoes and a missing hand. Over the cash register, framed pictures of an extremely chunky Elizabeth Taylor and an astonishingly young Shelley Winters hung beside a bulletin board filled with advertisements for Weight Watchers, dating services for heavy women, and various psychotherapists and self-help groups.

"Hello, Boris. Sorry I'm a little late," said Manya, letting the door slam behind her. A tinkling of bells echoed in the small shop.

"Why should you be sorry? Why do Americans apologize so much? Why are you a little late? I don't pay you to sleep," said Boris, her boss. His thick Russian accent and his thick Russian moods misled many people into thinking he meant the things he said when he did not. As a corollary, people thought that he was joking when he spoke in earnest.

"How can I make it up to you? Do you want coffee, doughnuts, a pint of my blood?" Manya hung up her coat. She was one of the few people who understood when Boris was teasing. She had to pay careful attention to the subtle signals of his body and voice, but Manya did not mind. So what if Boris was more work than most people? She had no other people in her life.

"How can you make it up to me? There's a good question. Let me think on this. How can a pretty young girl make it up to me?"

Manya, embarrassed, began to take inventory. She was not used to flirtation, and Boris flirted with every woman, from six to sixty, who entered the shop. It was for this purpose that he cultivated his accent; having emigrated from Kiev with his mother at the age of six, Boris spoke English with ease, Russian with effort, and Ukrainian not at all. He was one of those men who use unhandsomeness to advantage. Boris was nine years older and four inches taller than Manya, but no more than two pounds heavier. He had a pointy nose and chin and glistening, clever eyes, which gave him a slightly ferretlike look. He attempted to disguise this with a dark, well-kept Vandyke beard, but it only made his eyes appear narrower and brighter. His skin was so pale that it had a faint bluish sheen to it. He wanted to marry an American woman, he said, if he could only find one who would cook Russian food. He kept a bottle of vodka next to a book of Pushkin's poetry in a drawer under the cash register and considered himself a closet romantic.

Boris was a bit of a specialist when it came to womanizing. He had a gift for making women feel beautiful, particularly older women, heavy women, and women who were married and had two or more children. He never made love to a woman without falling in love with her a little, and he never ended a relationship without feeling a twinge of real regret. Whenever possible, he let the woman end the relationship, becoming increasingly moody and difficult until she gave up on him. He liked to take two-week breaks between affairs to build up an appetite. He had hired Manya in one of those dry spells, attracted by the shy way she scuffled into his shop on her moccasined feet. Manya was different from his other women. He felt that there was something grave and fine about the way she performed the smallest tasks—folding clothing, hanging up signs, ringing up a sale on the cash register. He would have liked to invent new words for the various qualities of her silences, just as the Eskimos had invented words for the various qualities of snow. He had the suspicion that if he seduced Manya, he could wind up falling deeply in love with her. A little bit in love, like a little bit of vodka, was all Boris thought a person needed to keep happy yet remain fit and alert—more than that was bad, even dangerous.

"So, Manya," Boris said, "tell me what you did last night."

"I think I met a Sally Shickelgruber," Manya replied.

"What's that?" Boris asked.

But she wouldn't explain herself.

SALLY SHICKELGRUBER

~

ho has not had a Sally Shickelgruber or an Adam Mandrake in their lives? At fourteen, when other girls are
gawky with innocence, the Sally Shickelgrubers of this world
are already feline with experience. Every boy in the class is in
love with Sally, except for Adam Mandrake, who is in love
with himself and already wears aftershave. Sally and Adam
date, but never for long. They are always making up or breaking up. Together they are the ruling couple; apart, they are
wolves among sheep.

At the end of Manya's freshman year in high school, Sally
invited the entire class to spend the weekend at the Shickelgrubers' summer house in Connecticut while her parents were
away in Paris. Sophie, unaware that the senior Shickelgrubers
would not be present, drove her daughter all the way to the
house, kissed her on the forehead, and told her that she
would come back for her on Sunday.

On Friday night at 9:00 p.m., while heavy rock music was
blasting from the stereo, Adam Mandrake broke up with Sally
Shickelgruber. At 9:30, he noticed that Manya had the largest
breasts in the ninth grade.

"Hi," said Adam, reeking of aftershave and baring white
teeth in a grin.

"Hi," Manya replied, surprised and gratified by this attention.

"Want to smoke a joint?"

"Sure," said Manya, feeling anything but sure. But a request
from Adam Mandrake was like a summons from the king; one

does not argue with the whims of royalty. He led her into a bedroom. The grass made her cough, and Adam told her shortly that she was not smoking it correctly. Manya apologized. After a few minutes she felt strangely disjointed, as if she had come down with a fever. Looking up, Manya saw a picture of a little girl sitting on her mother's lap. The mother's blonde hair was teased into a bouffant; otherwise, she looked exactly like Sally Shickelgruber. Adam tried to fondle one of Manya's large breasts through her crisp white shirt. In another room, someone laughed and said, "God, I'm trashed. Anyone seen my bra?" It was a carrying voice, throaty and sophisticated. Manya excused herself and walked out of the dark bedroom, through the smoke-filled living room where Sally Shickelgruber and five other people sat in various stages of undress, flipping quarters into a mug of beer. Manya made her way along the obstacle course of half-empty bottles, out the front door and along a dirt road until she reached the highway. She walked past cars which stopped and then drove on when she ignored them, until she reached the Starlight Motel.

"May I use your phone?" she asked the woman at the front desk.

"If you're staying," the woman replied, removing a pencil from her beehive hairdo.

Manya called collect. "Mom," she said, "I'm staying the night at the Starlight Motel, and then I want to take the bus back to New Jersey. I only have about thirty dollars on me. Could you wire me some money?"

"Manya," said Sophie on the other end. She was in shock. "Are you all right?"

Manya turned to the woman at the desk. "Do I look all right to you?"

"Sure," the woman said. "We get your type all the time."

Nothing in the room matched; the pattern on the rug clashed with the pattern on the wallpaper, the cheap painting of the clowns clashed with the colors of the bedspread. Manya took a long bath and cried. She had not eaten in twelve hours, but was too frightened to leave the safety of the motel. When she went to bed, she pulled the covers around her and listened, miserable, to the creaking of the bed in the room adjoining hers. The walls were so thin she heard the gasping "oh, oh" of the woman and the "Jesus, yes" of the man.

By the time Manya arrived at her mother's house in Maplewood, she had lost five pounds. She had not eaten any food at the motel in the event that she, like Persephone in Hades, would have to remain in hell if she dined on hell's offerings.

"Are you all right, Manya?" Sophie did not want to ask more than this. Her own mother had interrogated her constantly, and she'd promised herself to be different with her child.

"Just hungry, Mom." Manya remained hungry for a month. It felt to her as though a little tapeworm of misery drained all the pleasure out of food the instant she ate it, leaving her voracious, making her eat more.

When Manya topped the scale at one hundred and thirty-five pounds, she found that nothing in her closet fit her. Her stomach rumbled, constantly digesting, painfully distended. Manya was a prisoner inside her expanding body, a small unhappy voice in a large pale flabby cell. The first stretch marks appeared on her upper thighs and breasts.

Those breasts, always large but now positively overflowing, abundant to the point of absurdity, drew men's stares in the streets. Manya strapped herself into nursing bras—the only bras which now fit her—and attempted to hide in men's extra-large black T-shirts. But when a fourteen-year-old girl looks like a prehistoric fertility symbol and the weather is humid and sultry, the only safe place to hide is inside the cave.

Alone in the house with her hunger and her fat, bored and frightened at the prospect of real obesity, Manya discovered two things: that she could make herself throw up, and literature. She had heard about both before, of course, but never experienced them firsthand. Interestingly enough, in her mother's old *Concise Oxford Dictionary of Current English,* circa 1964, bulimia was described as (med.) morbid hunger, (fig.) voracity (for books etc.). Manya, who had previously eaten fattening foods but not binged, and had read the usual pubescent fare of assigned classics and paperback romances but no masterpieces, began to consume the contents of kitchen shelves and living room bookcases.

It goes without saying that Manya did not receive any more invitations from Sally Shickelgruber.

AN INVITATION FROM OPHELIA

~

A few days later, when Manya was standing in an extremely long line to buy textbooks, she met Ophelia again.

"You. I know you," said Ophelia. "How do I know you?"

Manya did not know what to say to this.

"Oh, I remember. The chocolate fiend. I liked you, didn't I?"

"I think you said something to that effect."

"There must have been a reason. Oh, well. My name's Ophelia. Like Hamlet's Ophelia. Do you think that's a strange name?"

"Not really. My name's Manya."

Ophelia laughed, delighted. "Now, that *is* a fine name. Mania. It means a specific type of madness, does it not? Man-i-a," she sang, a trifle off key, "I just met a girl called Man-i-a ..."

"Actually, it's pronounced like Tanya. Hey, look, I'm sorry if I was rude to you the last time we met," said Manya, who apologized frequently and with little provocation. "I was just in a foul mood, you know?"

"That's okay. I don't remember a bit of it, but if I know me, I was testing you." Ophelia smiled at Manya, a seductive smile in a face bare of makeup, from chapped and seemingly blood-less lips. She could have been a waif from the neck up, with her short fair hair ruffled into two owl-like tufts above the reddened tips of her ears. From the neck down, however, she resembled a hooker; a fake leopard-fur dress, not new, barely concealed the tops of her thighs.

"Testing me?" Manya stopped walking. "What for?" She was annoyed, and it showed. Like a porcupine, Manya used prickliness as her main defense; when threatened, she raised her chin and broadened her vowels, each gesture like the unfolding of a thin, razor-sharp quill.

"Testing your mettle. 'How should I my true love know from another one? By his cockle hat and staff and his sandal shoon.' Hamlet, act four, scene five. You pass, but barely—you do have a high doormat quotient, you know. Hey, what's that? An engagement ring?" Ophelia reached for Manya's left hand.

"Hardly. It's sort of a widowed ring. The Victorians used to make up these mourning rings after their husbands or fathers died."

"Weird. So that's actually someone's hair in the glass?"

"I guess so. I bought it in an antique shop because I felt sad for it. I mean, someone made this ring up to remember a person they loved, and here it is all these years later, gathering dust in a display case."

"That's macabre. That's fantastic. You wouldn't sell it to me, would you?"

"Sorry, I can't," said Manya proudly. She was glad to have Ophelia envy her something. Manya caressed the ring with her thumb. "Most people think it's disgusting."

"Not me. I'm a big fan of death. Death makes everything interesting, don't you agree? Oh, here, take this." Ophelia handed Manya a slip of blue paper.

"What is it?"

"It's an invitation to a party tonight."

A party! Manya was torn between pleasure and desperation. "I wouldn't know anyone there," she said.

"Dog testicles. You'll know me, and if you know me, all the obsequious rabble will pretend to know you."

This was not vanity on Ophelia's part; no one is so beloved in college as a chic little self-destructive vampire. Only in college could Ophelia display the thin scars on her inner wrists as if they were diamond bracelets.

"Well then," said Manya doubtfully, "maybe I'll come."

"Of course you will. I'll write my dorm room on the back of the invite so we can meet there first." Ophelia propped the invitation on Manya's arm, scribbled her address on it, and handed it back to her. The lettering resembled Gothic calligraphy.

"You have beautiful handwriting," Manya said.

"It looks better when I write in blood," replied Ophelia. Manya smiled. "I wasn't joking," Ophelia added.

Manya did not make a conscious decision to accept Ophelia's invitation; rather, she felt herself to be under some vague obligation. As she made her way toward Ophelia's dorm, Manya wondered if that had been Ophelia's intention. Bargains with the devil were traditionally signed in blood, weren't they?

Ophelia's room was identical to Manya's in architecture, but she had transformed it with magic, the kind of magic which seems perfectly ordinary to those who know how to arrange chairs and hang pictures and throw scarves over tables so that everything combines to give the impression of rightness and elegance. Mattresses were placed end to end over the entire floor, a mobile of stuffed animals and dolls' heads was strung over the doorway, and the entire front bumper of a car was affixed to the wall where it joined the ceiling. A large poster of a barren postnuclear landscape, taped to the window, read: RALLY ON DECEMBER 21 FOR THE DOOMSDAY COALITION.

"Hello, earth goddess," said Arthur by way of greeting. He was lying nude on one of the mattresses.

"Hello!" Manya's startled shout echoed in her own ears. "Sorry, I didn't see you. I mean, I didn't see you until just now. I was just looking for Ophelia—this is her room, I mean, is this her room?"

"Yes. Yes. Oh, absolutely yes." Arthur stood up, lean and decadently pale, and approached her. When he breathed, she noticed, his ribs stood out in bold relief. "She told me an earth goddess was due to make an appearance. I am your humble slave." Arthur lifted her hand and kissed it, and Manya, who had unthinkingly dropped her gaze out of modesty, inhaled sharply through her nose when she realized her mistake. She had never smelled a naked man before; this one had a clean, dry fragrance spiced with verbena. "You don't mind my worshipful nakedness? No disrespect intended, I assure you."

He must be gay, thought Manya. She felt as if she were in the presence of a young reincarnation of Oscar Wilde, and was put at her ease. "Earth goddesses expect this sort of thing," she said. She was learning to improvise.

"So where is Ophelia?" Manya sat down cautiously on a mattress.

"Oh, she's about. She'll be here, late as usual." Arthur, reclining again, propped his chin up with one fist.

"Yes." Manya looked around the room again. She wondered what kept the car bumper on the wall.

"Well, goddess, if you're bored with waiting, I don't suppose you want to give me a hand job until she arrives?"

Four years since someone had last propositioned her, a long dark path from the Starlight Motel. Manya's heart gave two hard raps against the inside of her chest, then steadied. Thump-thump. Thump-thump.

Manya gave Arthur a disdainful look and stood up to leave. She had gone two steps when Ophelia appeared at the door.

"Has Arthur been being a shit?" she asked cheerfully, and then laughed at Manya's expression. "That means he likes you, silly! He's polite to the people he hates, aren't you, asshole darling?"

"Whatever you say." Arthur covered his face with a pillow. "But I am uncomfortably horny," he added in a muffled voice.

Manya looked at the doorway, confused. Leave or stay? Would the evening get better or worse? Her heart was pounding again. She wanted to go back to her own room, to safety. Yet this was exciting, exciting and different.

"The goddess," she offered, "is not amused." Ophelia and Arthur applauded as if Manya were an actress making her debut. Manya felt better. She *was* learning to improvise. Already she felt like a slightly different person.

FEMINIST FANTASIES

~~

Bubbles, bubbles. After toil and troubles, Emilia Larsdatter sank into a bubble bath, the expensive herbal kind packaged according to its purported properties: soothing aloe, invigorating mint, healing lily milk, arousing musk. Emilia was trying for a feeling of romance, and so her bath was scented with jasmine—the sharpest of florals.

How is it that a day spent alone in avoidance of work can feel more enervating than a day spent chasing wild bison along the prairie? She'd been in her apartment all day, grading papers, planning classes, cleaning the bathroom, and otherwise avoiding what she was really supposed to be doing, namely reworking her doctoral dissertation. Emilia had been living with her dissertation for so many years that by now it felt more like a bad marriage than an academic enterprise. Heedless of her father's warning that her subject matter was too broad, Emilia had started out writing "The Imaging of Objectified Woman from Victorian Literature to Modern Popular Fiction."

Forced to acknowledge that she had neither the intellect nor the ambition to tackle such a topic, Emilia took a leave of absence from her studies and began working as a waitress in a small Greenwich Village Italian restaurant. It was at this restaurant that Emilia met Saul, whom she held solely responsible for her slender figure and partially responsible for her distrust of men. Saul was a very demanding man. He demanded that his linguine be al dente, that his water be ice cold, that he be given three months' credit for wine, and that Emilia have an affair with him. He was writing a poetry play, he said, and his art made certain requirements of him. Emilia, who served him limp pasta and lukewarm water and refused him wine without cash up front, could not resist the last demand. Their affair lasted for two memorable years, a period which Emilia liked to refer to as her prehistory. By this she meant that their relationship was not only over, but relegated to a distant and unfathomable past. In point of fact, however, their relationship was not exactly over. Like malaria, it recurred from time to time in uncontrollable fits.

After Saul's departure from her life—he decided that he needed to be in "the bardic atmosphere of Ireland" in order to finish his play—Emilia reentered Columbia. She revamped her thesis into a study of the image of objectified woman in Elizabeth Arkoway's *Flesh of Frailty*. As Arkoway was a Victorian writer so obscure that not one of Emilia's professors had actually read her, Emilia found that she had claimed an almost virgin territory. For the past six years Emilia had been trying to find a way to turn this paper into a book tentatively entitled "Woman: Love Object or Loved as Object?" So far, she had only managed to wrest two measly articles from her thesis, and two articles would not tenure achieve.

Emilia sat upright with a start, splashing herself. This was no good. Between thoughts of Saul and thoughts of tenure, she was becoming tense again. Sliding back down into the bath, Emilia shut her eyes and allowed her thoughts to drift.

What does a feminist English professor fantasize about? But Emilia was not a feminist English professor; that was simply her profession. Emilia was at an age which many consider to be a woman's sexual peak. She had a lovely body, albeit a little too thin in the breasts and rear. Her thick dark hair, prematurely streaked with silver in a little zigzag at her brow, reached the small of her back when it was not caught up in a bun. There were lines around her eyes and mouth, lovely sad lines which made some people think she must have been stunning as a young woman. Actually, age had cured her looks of blandness, given her spice.

In her fantasies, she was dressed in a forest-green gown, her waist corseted to seventeen inches in circumference, and she was cooking over a huge cast iron stove in a nineteenth-century farmhouse. There was a noise; who could it be? Two hillbillies, one short and fat, the other tall and broad. The fat one grabbed her, wheezing with laughter. Emilia reached behind her, found a green glass bottle, and broke it over his head.

"Get her, Varn," said the short hillbilly, sinking to his knees and passing out.

"Whoa, now," said Varn, pinioning her arms, then lifting her easily over one brawny shoulder. His long lank hair curled out from underneath a battered leather hat. His rough-spun shirt smelled of sweat.

"Let me go," screamed Emilia, and he did, but only after reaching her bedroom. Sprawling on the faded blue-and-white quilt, Emilia tossed until she had freed herself from her skirts.

"Quit fightin'," said Varn, holding her down. His lips brushed hers, oddly gentle.

Emilia started like a frightened doe; then she launched herself at Varn, kissing him wildly, openmouthed, tugging at his shirt until it ripped at the neck, exposing his shoulders. He kissed her back, hands tangling in her bun, unloosing her hair in a tumble of pins, releasing a burst of the jasmine scent she'd put in her shampoo ...

Fire burn and cauldron bubble. In olden times, the cauldron was a symbol for the womb, as Emilia well knew. She ran more hot water into the bath, pouring the herbal powder into the flow.

BIG RUSSIAN WOMEN
~

Boris had always prided himself on his ability to choose whom he would next fall in love with as easily as most people choose where they will next go on vacation. Recently, he had chosen to fall in love with a woman who seemed as eager for romance as she seemed incapable of sustained emotion. Her name was Vanessa and she had a career, which reassured Boris; his previous lover had tried to make Boris her career. The only problem was that Boris was having a bit of difficulty falling in love this evening. His mind kept wandering. Tomorrow morning, he thought, he'd have Manya get bagels and lox for their brunch. Or maybe he should go out to the deli for a change, to show Manya he trusted her alone in the store.

"I don't understand European men," said Vanessa, trying to get Boris's attention. "Russian men are European, aren't they?"

"I do not understand American women. Incomprehension is its own kind of charm. If we understood each other, we might find it boring," said Boris, noticing for the first time that his date's auburn hair was actually hennaed, and that her smile revealed a great deal of gum and an overbite.

"Oh, I don't know about that. I don't think you know how to be boring." Vanessa giggled, a sound which seemed incongruous coming from her long, slightly horsey face. She was having a very good time, listening to the murmur of Russian all around her, sipping champagne and eating from a frighteningly large assortment of appetizers. Boris and Vanessa's table was almost flush with the dance floor, where one chubby girl in a white sailor dress was yanking a toddler in a pink frilly jumper around and around. The band, which included a woman singer stuffed sausage-fashion into tight black satin pants, was playing a medley of Russian folk tunes.

"I can be boring, beleef me," said Boris, slavicizing his accent for effect. He speared a fat slice of kishke on his fork and waved it playfully in front of Vanessa's mouth.

"Oh, I couldn't," she demurred. "I'll get heavy."

"I *like* heavy," said Boris, his dark moist eyes pinning her gaze. "I like big Russian women," he added suggestively, smiling until the corners of his mouth seemed to disappear into his neat Vandyke beard.

"Do you really?" No sooner had Vanessa opened her mouth to speak than it was filled with kishke. She raised her napkin to her lips and chewed while Boris, leaning forward and resting his chin on one fist, watched.

There are no maps to chart the vast expanse between the

way people behave and what they feel. The only clues we have are the discrepancies of our own experience. How often have you smiled and seemed happily content but really been a roiling mass of insecurity? How many times have you said "I love you" and felt only the dull echo of doubt as consequence?

While Boris plied Vanessa with vodka and music and three different types of potatoes, he was not thinking about getting her into bed. Far from it. Boris was thinking about Manya, wondering if she had ever had a boyfriend, wondering if she would like kishke and how her mouth would look filled with kishke, wondering if he could manage to fall in love with Vanessa while wondering about Manya. Abruptly, Boris wondered why he was even wondering about falling in love with Vanessa. It was all right to question whether or not you *should* fall in love with someone, he thought, but it was bad news to be questioning whether you *could*. Did he need to feel in love with someone, preferably someone essentially unavailable, so that he could maintain his image of himself as a closet romantic while seducing as many women as he liked?

"Listen to that song," said Vanessa, by now finished chewing. "It sounds so gypsyish."

"Would you like to dance, my dear?"

"But there's no one else on the floor."

"Pish-tush. Let us show them how it is done." Boris's chair scraped against the floor, and he reached for Vanessa's hand. Ah, romance! It would be foolish of Boris to destroy the moment by admitting to his real thoughts. Besides, he had no way of knowing what Vanessa was really thinking as she smiled her buck-toothed smile and blushed and allowed him to lead her out onto the floor.

This is what Vanessa was thinking: *He isn't shrimpy at all. I never should have told Mildred that I'd dump him after an hour or so and join her for that party. Should I call Mildred and cancel? She did say that there'd be tons of single guys there, and single guys going for advanced graduate degrees at that. Maybe I'll just tell Boris I have a headache but I'll be very encouraging and we can make a date for tomorrow night, which is certainly better than sleeping with him right away. It's just like that Cosmo article said: "Men don't go the whole distance with women who go all the way right away."*

THE PARTY

~

There are those for whom parties are pleasure, and those for whom parties are grief. As Ophelia stood in front of a mirror lining her eyes with black makeup, pausing intermittently to drink vodka from a paper cup, Manya shivered with fear at the prospect of being crowded in among ebullient strangers. Arthur had gone to his own room to get dressed.

"I hope my hair isn't going to fall out from abuse," Ophelia was saying. "I had to try seven different shades of blonde until I hit on the idea of just using stripper."

"Stripper?"

"The thing you use to strip the color from your hair before adding sunshine blonde or champagne blonde or whatever. Only I didn't add anything." Ophelia finished with a smug nod of her head. She had the air of a scientist who has just explained a basic but heretofore undiscovered law of physics.

Lifting the tails of her best jacket so that she did not wrinkle it, Manya sat down on a chair. When Ophelia moved away from the mirror, Manya saw that it bore the legend COLLEGE IS A GIANT MATTRESS scrawled in purple lipstick.

"I've thought about dying my hair, but I was always scared it wouldn't suit me," said Manya. "Do you think I'd make a good blonde?"

"Why not? Change your look and you change your life," said Ophelia glibly, as if she were selling a line of products. "Never underestimate the power of a haircut. Ever notice how women always cut their hair when they're depressed? They tell themselves they're going for a new image, but really they're indulging themselves in an ancient mourning ritual that originated with the Egyptians."

"If I cut my hair every time I was depressed, I'd be bald."

"So you probably eat when you're feeling down. Oh, don't get offended," Ophelia said, waving her hand and inadvertently brushing her small breasts, which were exposed almost to the nipple in a strapless dark green gown. "Eating, cutting hair, it's all part of denying your attractiveness and hence your sexuality. I won't go on about it, though. You'll get enough lingo about repressed female sexuality in Professor Larsdatter's feminism class."

Manya felt exposed and abraded; Ophelia's catty remarks licked roughly over her nerves. Suddenly she realized what Ophelia had just revealed.

"You mean you're in that class, too? I haven't seen you there."

"I go incognito, in glasses and a scarf, so I won't be recognized later in the semester when I decide to cut. That's the way to do it. Besides, I know all Larsdatter's stuff by heart.

She's just a cheapo imitation of the French theorists." Ophelia spun around and moaned loudly. "I'm having an orgasm! I'm having a *jouissance* experience!"

"Are you really, my dear?" asked Arthur, appearing at the door garbed in black T-shirt, black jacket, and kilt.

"You got cigarettes?" Ophelia caught the pack of Camels one-handed and tapped it on her hip to shake a cigarette loose. "Men don't know the true orgasm, except for James Joyce. They live in their penises. We women have true, diffuse orgasms. That's what makes us better writers."

"Not more French feminist crap," said Arthur. "I thought you were over that unfortunate phase. We have a new project now."

"Do shut up. Are we ready to go, my love, my own?" Ophelia hooked her arm through Arthur's and looked at Manya over her shoulder. An unlit cigarette dangled from the corner of her mouth. "Come on, Dorothy. Time to leave Kansas."

The party was in married housing, five blocks away. The apartment was large, and filled with smoke and laughing faces and clinking glasses and sudden movements because something had spilled. A 1940s song was playing in the background, loudly enough so that when the deep baritone voice intoned, "Why do the trees have to know?" several people were startled out of their conversations.

"God," said Ophelia. "Mating season among the mastodons."

"I'll see what I can do about the music," Arthur said, and disappeared.

Manya stood rooted to one spot and wondered what to do with her hands. She had always envied people who could adopt a casual pose in the center of a crowded floor, temporarily alone, letting their eyes roam casually over the room as if selecting from a tray of human appetizers. This was what Ophelia was doing. Manya, on the other hand, felt like a child lost in the middle of a department store, and it took all her attention to keep her left eye from twitching. Should she hold her hands in front of her, or did that look too defensive? If she got a drink, which would solve the problem of hands, would she lose Ophelia in the process?

"Mish-Mish," Ophelia said, waving a hand at a young man in a faded brown corduroy jacket. He had an unruly mane of dark brown hair, a chin shaped like a shovel, and fierce black eyes half hidden behind bulky black-framed glasses. "Darling, we have to speak. How's life among the radicals? I hear the upcoming rally's going to be the biggest thing at Columbia since '68. Do you think any buildings will be seized, or is that too done already?"

"What the hell are you talking about?" asked Misha, his eyes blazing—with some unnamed fervor or merely with irritation—behind his spectacles.

"Where have you been, Mish? I thought you were in on campus politics. I was sure you were the person to ask." Sensing that her companion was losing patience, Ophelia said quickly, "I'm talking about the Doomsday Coalition rally. I would've thought you were involved, considering the scope of the thing. Good lord, the media's going to be there and everything."

"The Doomsday Coalition?" Misha's skin, which was rough in texture, pocked and cratered, gave him an appearance of greater age and experience than he actually possessed. It was the perfect attribute for a would-be revolutionary: flesh that had weathered internal storms of hormones, flesh that seemed to have suffered.

Ophelia laughed, a light and unforced peal of mockery. "You're not going to tell me you haven't heard of them, are you, Mish? I thought they'd gotten to everyone. It's right up your alley—a coalition of professional pessimists. Every underground anarchist, every environmentalist, at least five political scientists ..." Ophelia paused and took a breath. "Every New Age prophet, half the AIDS activists, all the nuclear alarmists—particularly the nuclear alarmists—and assorted artists and writers." Ophelia smiled and lit the cigarette she had been holding in her hand.

"Interesting. Suspiciously vague, but interesting. So when is this supposed coalition planning their supposed rally?"

"After finals, of course. Oh, don't look at me like that! It has to be right around Christmas, when everyone's celebrating the holy birth. What better time for a carnival of death to warn people of the imminent dangers facing our planet? Oh! Keegan!" Ophelia waved imperiously at someone across the room. Then she elbowed her way into the throng, and was gone. Misha looked after her with an inscrutable expression. Then he, too, drifted away.

Manya, like Misha, had been listening with interest and some suspicion. Now she wondered if she should follow Ophelia. Or would that make her appear ridiculous? She veered toward the kitchen instead, where there were six people crammed together, speaking too softly for her comfort. Manya managed to find an unopened can of beer by someone's elbow.

"That's probably warm," said a tall, chunky woman with red hair. She was standing off to one side, an amazon with broad hips and thighs, dressed in a conservative pastel plaid skirt. She was in her late twenties.

"I can't brave trying for the refrigerator," said Manya gratefully. She was speaking to someone; she was visibly in conversation.

The amazon, equally glad to be lifted from the gutter of party solitude, burst into rapid-fire speech. "I find this kind of thing a bit too much for me nowadays. You know, I had a dinner date tonight, but I had to leave early because I was invited to this party by a friend who's in business school at Columbia. But I don't see Mildred anywhere." The amazon looked around. "Everyone here seems awfully young. Maybe she left already. I should never have told her I would come."

Manya, gulping her beer, silently agreed with this sentiment. A sudden fierce thumping from the stereo was followed by a blare of rhythmic, synthesized sound. An approving murmur from the crowd greeted this development. In the other room, feet began to pound against the flat gray industrial carpet.

"Oh, by the way, what's your name? Mine's Manya."

"Glad to meet you, Manya. I'm Vanessa." They shook hands, then watched as some of the kitchen crowd moved into the living room. "Do you want to dance?" asked Vanessa.

"Not really."

"Good. I hate dancing," said Vanessa. "I always feel so undignified with my arms and legs flailing about. My date danced with me earlier this evening, and that was all right, couple dancing. But when I'm on my own, I wind up stepping on someone's feet, or elbowing them by accident. And I hate the thought of all my flesh jiggling."

"Me too. I think it's being large," said Manya, seized with an urge to speak frankly.

Manya had drunk almost the entire can of beer on an empty stomach, but it was not alcohol which stirred her to speech. It was the atmosphere. All that chanting, repetitive music! All those bodies spinning and writhing! No revival tent could have been more hypnotic.

"But you're not large," said Vanessa, towering over her. "Oh, you mean large as in overweight large! I hadn't thought of that. You mean you feel self-conscious about moving around on the dance floor? But at least you're not massively tall, like me."

"Maybe not, but what jiggles on me isn't supposed to jiggle," said Manya. She felt exhilarated. It seemed to her that they were like two underground Jews, surrounded by the Spanish Inquisition, taking a chance on the truth.

"Oh, there you are," said Arthur. "Have you heard about the rally?"

Manya spun around, only to realize that he was talking to someone with a Dutch-boy haircut and a vacant expression.

"The doomsday thing?" Dutch-boy nodded. "Personally, I think it's all a lot of bullshit. Don't you?" There was something obsequious about his manner; Manya decided that she disliked him.

Arthur's eyes narrowed, and his face took on an almost saturnine expression. "Not at all," he said. "I think it's marvelous. You see, I approve of anything to do with the imminent annihilation of the human race. Destroy and rebuild."

"Who's the yummy blond guy?" asked Vanessa.

"I think he's taken," said Manya, searching the room for a glimpse of Ophelia. Manya spotted her standing in a corner with her back up against the wall, flirting with three different partners who were all laughing in the manner of soldiers in somebody else's country. Straining to hear over the incessant hum of the crowd, Manya caught snatches of their conversation.

"Doomsday Coalition."

"Don't you think it's all a big put-on?"

"I've heard of them—they're actually a coven here on campus. They've been a secret society for over fifty years. You only find out about them if they choose you as an initiate."

Manya realized that other people around her were also discussing the rally. For a moment it seemed to her that the general din of music and conversation had become a single droning noise, as if from a vast hive of bees, a palpable vibration that was both alarming and unpleasant.

"Are you planning on going soon?" she asked her companion. "We could leave together."

"Sure. If we leave now, I could always try calling my date and telling him my headache's better."

EVEN A LITTLE IN LOVE

~

Even a little in love hurts. It is a small pain that pounces suddenly; ask Boris. There he was, lying in bed with Vanessa, her head pillowed on his shoulder, and then—pow! He thought of Manya and where she might be at that very moment, and a twinge, like a muscle spasm, hit him. Well, why not? The heart is a muscle, after all.

"What's the matter?" asked Vanessa, raising her head a little so that she could look at him. After leaving the party at Columbia she had telephoned Boris to tell him that her headache was gone. He'd said he was glad to hear it. She'd told him that she realized she'd been afraid of her own attraction to him, but that she now accepted her feelings. She said this so convincingly that she believed it herself. They had spent an athletic and enjoyable night at Boris's apartment, but now it was morning, and Vanessa was experiencing severe postcoital anxiety.

"Nothing's wrong. What makes you think something's wrong?" As Boris stroked her hennaed hair, he concluded that she was a bit too heavy to be lying on him like that. Vanessa had thick long limbs and a clumsy way of arranging them. Manya, by contrast, was petite and rounded and feminine. Boris thought her head would feel like a small kitten curled up on his shoulder. Vanessa's head felt like a rock.

"Sorry, am I crushing you? God, will you look at my hair, it'll take hours to get the tangles out, not that I mind, you sexy devil, you. It's not really red, you know. My sister Jenny got the red hair in the family."

"How many children were you in your family?" Boris reached for a cigarette. He did not really care about what he was saying; by the time Vanessa replied, he had half forgotten his question. What was the matter with him? He was experiencing none of the sensual delight he usually felt in the aftermath of sex . He wished he could get up and wash. He wished he could get up and remove his skin.

"Three of us girls," said Vanessa, happy to reminisce for her lover. She took this as a sign of his interest in continuing their relationship. "Marian's married with two kids, and Jenny just got married a month ago." Vanessa leaned over and kissed Boris. "Maybe it's time for me to think about getting married, too." She giggled, and gave him a playful nip on the ear to show that she was only kidding.

"*Bozshe moi*. Is it that time already?" asked Boris, sitting up and drawing the sheet over his naked lap. He shut his eyes and tried to sort out the confusing parade of emotions marching through his aching head. There, that was guilt over there. No mistaking that heavy footfall. But the small one skulking in the corner, what was that? No, it couldn't be.

Vanessa put her hand on his shoulder. "Boris," she said huskily.

"I have to get up and go to the work."

"I think I'm falling in love with you."

"It's annoying, but what can I do?" Boris tugged his pants on.

"It's annoying that I love you!"

Boris stopped. "No, no, not annoying, that's not the word. It's ..." Sometimes, in awkward moments, Boris's normally fluent English would founder on the rocks of emotion. Perhaps it was because he was used to speaking broken Russian while feeling intensely. He reverted to his mother tongue when in the throes of passionate grief or happiness for two reasons: because he thought it a more expressive language, and because his lovers never understood what he had said, and therefore could not throw it back at him later.

Forced to reply to Vanessa in English, Boris struggled for an appropriate word.

"Inconvenient. Yes, it is inconvenient."

"It's inconvenient that I love you?"

"No, no. It is inconvenient that I have to go to work, not that you love me." He resumed dressing. "And you don't love me, not really. It's just one of those things that pop into your mind after making love. All kinds of things pop into your mind, thoughts of love, disease, pregnancy ..." Boris, realizing what he was saying, turned around and kissed Vanessa reassuringly on the forehead.

"I guess you want me to leave?" she asked plaintively. Boris was almost entirely dressed now.

"I wish I could stay here and make love to you all day," Boris lied, "but I do have to work." That much was true.

"You hate me. I should have waited. If I'd waited, we might have had a chance." By now, Vanessa was convinced that she was in love. She had felt wonderful in Boris's arms, she felt terrible now that he was rejecting her—what more proof did she need? Vanessa was prone to attributing important causes to trivial effects. Every month just before her period, when her spirits flagged, she racked her brains for the reason her life was so terrible.

"Vanessa," Boris said, "you aren't in love. You just believe that you're in love. There's a difference."

"No, there's not," she said, sniffling. "Isn't there a quote somewhere that says, 'Love is half belief, half make-yourself-believe'?"

"Theodor Reik. He said, 'Romance is thus an alloy, composed of precious metal and some less pure. It is half love, half lie, half belief, half make-oneself-believe.'" Boris sat down on the bed, hard. Now he knew what that diminutive emotion at the back of the parade was. Ouch! His head ached worse than ever, not to mention his heart, but no real Russian romantic believes in pleasure without pain. Pain is like salt, giving love its savor, preserving it when it would otherwise prove perishable, feeding a hunger and creating a thirst.

"I'm in love," he said wonderingly.

"Boris!"

"But I'm not in love with you." As a womanizer, he had been kind, thinking of the other person's feelings, stepping carefully. As a lover, he was cruel, for he could only think of his own feelings, and of Manya's.

And Vanessa, who would have gotten over Boris very quickly had he simply gone on seeing her, promptly burst into tears, and the pain and salt of it preserved her love like brine.

TRUTH OR CONSEQUENCES

~~

Manya was a good salesperson. She never inflicted her opinions when they were not requested, and she avoided touching seams while they rested on hip or stomach or bust, for she knew that women, particularly heavy women, know when something is too tight and do not need someone to tug at the offending garment to drive the point home. When Manya had to reach over and pull up a zipper, she acted as if her hands were small blind diligent servants, unconnected to her person. She knew from her own experience that unfamiliar mirrors reflect flaws which familiar mirrors do not, and when her customers became upset, she knew which words would bring comfort. Manya saw herself as a guide, leading stumbling pilgrims through the rocky places where truth was sharp-edged and dangerous.

But for some reason, on this Sunday morning, there were no customers in the store.

"Manya," said Boris, propping his feet up on the front desk, "let's play a game."

"I'm not very good at games," she said, looking up from her book. She was perched precariously atop a high stool.

"This is a game anyone can play. It's called Truth or Consequences."

"We ask each other questions, and if one of us doesn't

want to answer we have to take a dare?"

"That's it," said Boris.

"You must be joking," said Manya.

"I am paying you," he reminded her.

"All right, then. Shoot." Manya folded her hands in her lap and regarded Boris with tolerant amusement. Two days ago, she would have hesitated at the prospect of revealing herself, but after the experience of Arthur and Ophelia, she felt like being a little daring.

"What sort of man could you fall in love with?"

Manya considered. "He would have to be trustworthy," she said, "but he would also have to be exciting and excitable. Someone sensitive and intelligent, who reads a lot, but also someone who has seen the world. I don't think he would need a sense of humor so much as a sense of the absurd. Oh, and he should have a few theories. I like people who have theories. All in all, a rogue, but an honest one. The best example I can think of would be Jack Tanner in Shaw's *Man and Superman*. Have you read it?"

"Don't change the subject. It's your turn, Manya. You ask me something."

"Okay. Hmm. All right, same question. What sort of woman could you fall in love with? Wait, I forgot, maybe I should ask you what sort of woman you couldn't fall in love with." Manya laughed until she saw that Boris was not laughing with her.

"The kind of woman I could fall in love with—I mean really fall in love with—is sitting right in front of me."

Manya was speechless, but only for a moment. "Boris, that's really unfair of you. Just because there's no one in the store today you try to finesse me, of all people. Take it back," she demanded playfully.

"I can't."

"Take it back!" She was becoming flustered.

"I can't take it back. It's the truth. Last night I was making love to someone and I couldn't stop seeing your face."

"That's disgusting!" Not to mention frightening. She imagined Boris imagining her face while making love to some other woman. It was a startlingly intimate thought, as if he'd made love to her without her knowing it. Manya's palms began to sweat. She'd felt a kind of pride in being the sole platonic female friend of a known womanizer. It had been like feeding a wild animal and knowing that the animal would rend anyone else to shreds. Now the animal had turned on her, and though she knew it was no more than his nature, Manya felt betrayed.

Boris walked over to Manya and took her hand in his. A memory of Arthur taking her hand to kiss it last night intruded, and Manya felt dizzy and slightly ill. Could Boris feel that her palms were damp? Why was everything becoming so complicated? At least Arthur had stated openly what he wanted. Boris was far more of a threat, because she had grown fond of him. What should she say? What could she do?

"Manya," said Boris, very gently. "I wouldn't do anything to frighten you."

But he was, he was! Manya pulled at her hand. "No, I know that. Please. Let go." Her lapdog face was pale and distraught, which, oddly enough, granted it a measure of beauty it rarely possessed.

"Manya. May I ..."

Ding, went the front door. In walked Vanessa.

"Vanessa!" said Boris. "What are you doing here?"

"Manya!" said Vanessa. "What are you doing here?"

"I work here," said Manya, extricating her hand from

Boris's. She turned to him in some confusion. "How do you know Vanessa?"

"I might ask the same thing."

Vanessa took a step toward her lover. "Manya and I met at a party last night. That's why I left the restaurant so early. I had to go, you see, because I'd promised a friend. But I came back, didn't I? I *wanted* to be with you."

"Your date last night was with Boris?" Manya struggled to assimilate this information. Her mind was not working properly. "The date you went dancing with?"

Boris, who had found Vanessa inconvenient a few hours before, was now truly annoyed with her. "After our date, when you said you had a headache, you went to a party with Manya?"

"Not *with* her. I only met her there. But I came back to you. I spent the night with you. And what's going on between the two of you, I'd like to know!"

"You spent the night together," said Manya. "Then she's the woman you said you were with when ..." Manya could not go on.

"Yes, we spent the night together. And then he said he had to go to work." Suddenly Vanessa's tone lost its sharp edge. "He said ... he had to go to work and that he was in love with someone else."

Vanessa and Manya looked at each other for a long moment, their faces wearing almost identical expressions of puzzlement and sadness.

Boris hoped that someone would recover and scream at him. He was experiencing intolerable levels of guilt.

"If it's you he's in love with, Manya, then I suppose I'll have to be noble about it," said Vanessa with only a trace of bitterness. "I can't dislike you. You're a very nice person." Vanessa thought for a moment. "Although perhaps I'd be doing you a favor if I didn't let you have him. He's hardly trustworthy."

"Trustworthiness is one of my prerequisites," said Manya. "And I certainly don't want anything to do with someone who would spend the night with you and then declare himself in love with me. I wonder where you'd be, Boris, if you'd spent the night with me? Declaring love to Vanessa?"

"That's ridiculous," said Boris. "Stop talking this way, both of you. This isn't some nineteenth-century English drawing room drama."

"I have always suspected," said Vanessa, "that life was a lot more like nineteenth-century English drawing room drama than anyone imagined."

"So have I," said Manya with surprise. "At least, I hoped it was."

"I've never liked the English," said Boris. "They have too much control and too little passion, as far as I'm concerned. I prefer weeping and shouting and having the whole thing out and over with. I don't like having to read between the lines."

"But that's where all the interesting stuff is, Boris," said Vanessa, turning on her heel and shutting the door behind her so gently that the bells dangling from the knob did not sound her exit.

After Vanessa left, customers arrived as if on cue. First an opera singer made an entrance. Next, a group of Orthodox Jewish women from Brooklyn came in, arguing amongst themselves and all needing dresses for the wedding of the rabbi's son. Then three large tourists from Texas jostled their way into the store, exclaiming good-naturedly over the city's dirt and the homeless situation. There was a heated theological discussion, for the Texans, who had "great admiration for the Chosen People," did not understand "how anyone could read the New Testament and not accept Jesus into their heart." The Jewish women tried to explain themselves but were interrupted by the opera singer, who managed to insult both groups by calling all organized religions "the solace of little spirits."

Eventually, when the store was empty again and the echo of dispute hung heavy in the air, Boris and Manya had to contend with each other.

"Manya, if you'll let me explain about Vanessa ..."

But Manya had recovered from her shock and was prepared. "You don't owe me any explanations, Boris. The way I see it, we should try to gloss over the unfortunate events of this morning."

"You mean you'll try to overlook the little fact of my being in love with you as if it were a wart that happened to have grown on my nose overnight?"

"It's not a wart. It's more like a birthmark. You were born with the compulsion to seduce every female you meet. You're just not used to the idea of being friends with a woman. I mean, look at me, Boris. I'm not exactly the kind of woman to inspire wild passion."

"What if I've had enough of wild passion? Perhaps I'd like some domesticated passion," said Boris half-jokingly. Then he turned serious. "I've never felt this way before. You're the only woman who has ever made me feel tender."

"Boris, that feeling is called affection. It's a lovely feeling. Dog people feel it for their dogs, and cat people for their cats. Between two human beings, it generally signifies friendship."

"Friends. All right. Friendship is a good place to start. For now we're friends. But if you do happen to discover that you're in love with me, we'll renegotiate our relationship. How's that?" Boris twinkled at her.

"First let me buy you a cat or a dog," said Manya.

OBEDIENCE TRAINING
~~

It is the custom of dog trainers to maintain that their methods are the most effective and their theories the most comprehensive. They will tell you that you must adhere rigidly to their system; they will explain to you why other systems don't work. Academics hold a similar view of their area of expertise. Professors will insist that their method of analyzing *Ulysses* is the only method which will really bring the material to heel; they will rub your nose in other theories and then disprove them until not even a whiff of someone else's opinion remains in the room.

Professor Larsdatter turned to Manya. "So, Ms. Mittelman, what is your opinion about this passage?"

Manya's opinion was that the passage had gone off on a tangent, but she was not going to admit to this. Professor Larsdatter had made no secret of her fondness for the opening paragraph of the chapter. "I felt that the author was trying to get us to feel for the heroine's dilemma by drawing a parallel between her forced marriage to the viscount and the fox caught in the trap."

"Let's elevate the level of this discussion," snapped Professor Larsdatter. "How about you, Ms. Saunders?"

Ophelia cleared her throat. "In this passage, the text reverts to the passive voice whenever it refers to the heroine or the vixen," she offered. "Clearly, there is a connection between the two, but the nature of that connection is a bit tricky. A closer reading of the text reveals that the words 'penetrated,' 'tearing,' 'pulsating,' and 'throbbing' are used to describe both the plight of the heroine and that of the vixen."

"Very good," said Emilia, pacing the room in her high heels: clickety-clack, clickety-clack. "The heroine loses her virginity and the vixen loses her leg. Sexual imagery crops up in the section about the vixen, and death imagery abounds in the sex scene between the heroine and the viscount. Guttering candles! Dying flowers! Some of my male contemporaries feel that a somewhat gothic sensibility has intruded on the text," she said, twisting her red mouth into a wry smile. "But I feel certain that we can sense a clear hint of irony here. Much as I hate to mention any biographical elements, or to refer to an author's intentionality—which is an iffy business, at best ..." Here Emilia sent Manya a quelling look.

Ophelia passed Manya a note. Manya unwrapped it carefully, and discovered an exquisite portrait of Professor Larsdatter, her forehead wrinkled in concentration, sitting on the toilet. But what good did that attempt at humor do Manya, whose intelligence, like a formerly well-behaved dog, was now doing everything wrong in front of its new trainer? She pulled, and her intelligence would not budge; she told it to come, and it went out into the field to play.

There are as many ways to train a dog as there are to read a book, of course, but tell that to an insecure eighteen-year-old. Manya did the best she could; she took scrupulous notes during the rest of the class, and spent the rest of the week either in the library or in her room, studying.

DANGEROUS PASTIMES

~

Contrary to popular belief, the young do not think that they are immortal. They do think that they are immune to death, and in a way, they are right. Life clings thickly to them, a double-strength membrane, cushioning them from blows that would kill a mature adult in an instant. Just as the pressure of the birth canal would crush a fully formed skull to bits but only bends an infant's head into an oblong shape which eventually corrects itself, adolescence bends the young but does not break them—at least, most of the time it doesn't. What happens to the unlucky, you ask? Maybe, like Icarus, they fly a little too close to the sun, or maybe they look down and forget to flap. Sometimes, like Phaëthon, they borrow their father's chariot and find that driving the sun through its circuit across the sky is harder than it looks. Still, it's amazing what the young manage to do without self-destructing. Tabs of acid taken once, twice, twelve times, on a hill, on a subway, in the middle of a crowded rock concert! Cocaine flooding up the nose, through the brain, into the pounding heart, while the body dances furiously on a stage filled with strangers! Mild narcotics smoked every day before Geometry while the brain is still developing! How tempting to forget that they are immune to death—at least, most of the time—and ask, Hey, where are you headed?

"Hey, Manya! Where are you headed?"

Manya, who had been halfway across Broadway, turned around and walked back to where Ophelia and Arthur stood, identically dressed in torn jeans and thick black sweaters.

"I haven't seen you since Monday," Ophelia said.

"That's because you cut Larsdatter's class on Wednesday and Friday."

"True enough. Well, come along with us now," said Ophelia. Her hair, lit by the afternoon sun, seemed like a pale flame. It was a very clear, bright day.

"Where are you going?"

"Just around here," said Arthur. "A little errand. By the way, where did you get to at that party? We missed you."

A pleasant little jolt to Manya's self-esteem, that. They'd missed her. "You two seemed busy enough," she said. "How's the Doomsday Coalition coming along?"

Ophelia grinned. "What a wise child we have, Arthur," she said. "Most people think it's a joke, but it's still a hot topic of conversation. That's phase one—plant the seed. Misha, everyone's favorite anarchist, is already seeing it as a golden opportunity. He likes the idea of formless protest. Phase two is outreach to professors—I see Larsdatter as nearly ripe. I've heard through the grapevine that tenure meetings start soon and she's walking a thin rope. Once we have her in the bag, we can start thinking media attention."

"You don't mind my asking what the ultimate goal of all this is, do you?" Manya was absurdly flattered at being taken into their confidence. To be in on someone else's secret is one of the deepest pleasures humans know, and one Manya had seldom experienced.

"Media and crowd manipulation. Training for our future, you might say. Also, to raise a little hell. College is particularly boring these days. In addition, we get to make fools of a lot of people. Most people are creeps and sycophants," said Ophelia. "But look, we'll miss our appointment. Want to join us?"

"Where are you going?" asked Manya for the second time.

"Just there." Arthur pointed across the street to a building which, when first built, might have been quite attractive. Now the stone grotesques perched over the entrance were blackened by grime and gave the edifice a sinister aspect. "It won't take long," said Arthur. "Besides, if you want to be part of the Doomsday Coalition, you have to attend organizational meetings. You've already missed quite a few, you know." Arthur took her hand and tucked it in the crook of his elbow. "My lady," he said. He offered Ophelia his other arm.

"So? Off to see the wizard," sang Ophelia, off key.

The lobby was large and dimly lit; at one time, a doorman might have greeted visitors. Now there was a buzzer system and an elaborate lock on the outer door, but both were broken.

"This doesn't seem very safe," said Manya as the elevator door slid shut. The conveyance grumbled beneath their feet at every floor they passed.

Arthur sniffed. "Smells like someone shat in here."

"Oh, shut up complaining," said Ophelia, almost maternally. "And remember, try not to talk when we get inside."

"Like I've never done this before!"

"She's my connection. You're just along for the ride. And some protection."

Manya stood listening quietly. This was not what she had expected. She did not know exactly what she'd expected, but it definitely was not this. She felt a frisson of something vaguer and more pervading than fear tickle the back of her mind, something like the darkness that falls across the path of fairy tale heroines. Why had she traveled so far from the safety of home? The woods were full of moving shadows and strange sounds. Home, home, safety, home. But like a fairy tale heroine, Manya was compelled by her own story line to keep her feet on the path to the evil witch's abode. When we are in the middle of our own tales, we tend to forget that we can break with convention, turn around, walk off the path, find a map, ask for directions.

"Scared?" asked Ophelia.

"Observing," said Manya. But she did not discount her feeling of foreboding.

Ophelia, Arthur, and Manya got out on the seventh floor. The paint had peeled off the walls in strips, but the hallway was no worse than many others. The door to the apartment they were looking for was plastered with *Sesame Street* stickers. Ophelia rang twice.

"Who is it?" The voice was a woman's, young and faintly accented.

"Me, Ophelia. And two friends. They're okay."

The door swung open, revealing a dark-haired, slender woman with ratlike features: long, sharp nose, darting, cautious, intelligent eyes. A slack-mouthed toddler perched on her angular hip. "Yeah? Come in," she said. The apartment behind her was ordinary in its squalor: clumps of dirty laundry on the chairs, broken plastic trucks on the floor, a soap opera blaring in Spanish from an unseen television set in another room. An older woman shouted something in Spanish, her plump form moving across an open doorway at the periphery of Manya's vision.

"That's my mother," said the rat-faced woman. She put the toddler down. "Go to Grandma," she commanded. It stared at her, and she pushed it gently in the right direction. Clumsily, it waddled off, peering over its shoulder at the strangers, a thin line of drool glistening on its plump lips.

"Lovely child," offered Manya reflexively.

"Isn't he?" Rat-face beamed. "He's very bright. Talks up a storm, usually, but he's had a little cold. Well, then. Come into the kitchen."

Manya thought, Maybe the child is very bright. For all we know, in years to come, he'll write novels about his peculiar home life.

"Here's the money," said Ophelia.

"Great." Rat-face sat down and began weighing a bag of white powder on a small scale. Arthur watched, and Manya was gratified to see that he, too, appeared nervous. Only Ophelia and Rat-face seemed completely at their ease.

"There you go," said the woman, handing Ophelia the bag. "I gave you a little extra," she added, smiling at Manya.

Manya flushed. She wished the woman would not look at her; she hoped the woman would not remember her face.

Just then, the grandmother appeared at the door with the toddler on her hip. Her broad features registered distaste. She said something in Spanish. Her daughter replied, somewhat sullenly, somewhat placatingly.

"We'll be going now," said Ophelia.

"It was nice to meet you," said Manya.

"Ma'am. Ma'am." Arthur gave a correct little nod to the older woman, and then to her daughter, but the tight ironic smile he wore made the gesture almost insulting.

"Whew," said Ophelia once the elevator door closed in front of them.

"Thanks for inviting me," said Manya in a small voice. She had meant it to sound ironic.

"My pleasure," said a voice from behind. Arthur, Manya, and Ophelia turned their heads at the same moment. There, in the corner, was a tall, gaunt, bearded young man in jeans too faded and dirty for fashion, or even antifashion.

The stranger leaned forward and sniffed the air near Arthur's face. "Been shopping for a party?"

Arthur reached forward to press a button and open the elevator door, but the stranger whistled warningly. Suddenly Arthur's face appeared very pale and effeminate next to the stranger's thick layer of dirt and dark facial hair.

"Hey, Bleach-boy, it's rude to leave without a word to the host. And I believe I just asked you a question. Maybe I should rephrase it." The stranger adjusted the crotch of his jeans, as if to accommodate unusually large genitals, or a weapon. Manya and Ophelia looked at Arthur. In the foxholes, they say, there are no atheists. Everybody falls back on tradition. Manya's and Ophelia's looks said: You're the man, do something!

"Great," said Arthur.

"What's great, Bleach-boy?"

"Whatever you said. A fine idea." Arthur was a modern man. He was comfortable with emotions, the few he had, comfortable with fear in particular. He was not about to die doing something brave.

Ophelia grunted with disgust. Then she drew herself up and faced the stranger with a peculiar glint in her eye. She was not very pretty at that moment; the full force of her vampiric nature gleamed out of her eyes with preternatural intensity. She bared her teeth in a baboon smile, panting a little high in her chest.

"You," she said. "What do *you* want?"

"Whaddaya think?" The stranger smiled.

Ophelia kept staring at him. She unveiled her eyes and

let madness peer out of them. "Do you think you're crazier than me?" she asked. "I doubt it. I hate men. I loathe and despise men."

"Well, he's a man, isn't he?" the stranger asked, pointing at Arthur. A polite, conversational question.

"Maybe I'll hurt you," said Ophelia, equally conversational. "There's three of us, and you look pretty weak to me."

"What if I have a knife?"

Suddenly it was apparent that beneath the dirt and hair, the stranger was quite young; sixteen, seventeen at most.

"What if you don't?" Ophelia turned to Arthur. "Press the button, asshole, and let this little shit out."

"Aw, c'mon. I could've killed you. You could at least gimme some of what you got."

The elevator door opened with a whine. "Get out, asshole," she said. The stranger left, looking sullen.

Manya turned around and stared at Ophelia. "You could have gotten us all killed!"

"Don't be a dip," said Ophelia. But Arthur was staring at her, too.

Children, do not attempt this trick at home, say all the television programs, but still the children do. Sometimes youth's double-strength membrane, that invisible safety net, ruptures and breaks. Parents cry and consult the experts and wonder why their children insist on courting disaster at every turn. Don't despair, parents; it's probably all part of nature's plan. The young of every species are the likeliest to be swallowed up by their environment. Baby crocodiles get eaten in the egg by lizards they would devour if fully grown. Lion cubs get mauled by jackals they would sneer at if they'd lived long enough.

"Why are you looking at me like that? Jeez, you guys are uptight." But Arthur and Manya continued looking. Their madness, or youth, or immunity to death—whatever you call it—was not so durably designed as hers, and this little scene had punctured their certainty. Suddenly Arthur and Manya were united, and Ophelia stood on the outside, uncomprehending.

"Why are you looking at me like that?" she asked again. They said nothing.

ARTHURIAN LEGEND

~

The persona Arthur wore at college was that of a decadent artistic sort who has no particular talent but possesses the arrogant rudeness associated with talent. It was a costume which suited him admirably, and fit him almost without gaps or wrinkles, but if you looked closely enough you might perceive bits of helpful padding here and there, and if you pulled down the zipper, an entirely different Arthur would emerge.

Arthur had managed to lose his accent, but could not rid himself of the slightly foreign rhythm which crept into his speech. He pretended that this was an affectation, and it would have required a very careful listener to guess otherwise. A slight glottal emphasis here, a guttural resonance there—a trained linguist might have made an accurate guess. It takes years to rinse out the flavor of a mother tongue.

Arthur was born to a German mother and a Jewish father.

In 1966, his mother, Heidi, had rebelled against her father and run off to Israel to volunteer on a kibbutz deep in the Negev desert. She worked in the date fields, supervised by an Israeli boy only a year older than she. His name was Aron.

Heidi was blonde and slender and reserved; Aron was barrel-chested and dark and exuberant. They fought until they made love one night when the full moon dropped low in the sky, like a birth about to happen. It was true love; even the planets knew it, and moved like eager dancers into auspicious constellations. Of course, the planets or the gods or whatever had to throw in some tragedy, just the right amount of pain to keep the brew potent over the years. So Aron went to war in 1967 and lost a leg, and Heidi proved unable to conceive. The doctors said it would take a small miracle for her ever to become pregnant.

But who deserved a miracle more than Heidi and Aron? Aron felt sure the child would be special; all the heroes of the Bible were born when divine intervention opened their mothers' formerly barren wombs. When Arthur was born, they named him Barak, but Heidi kept seeing her father's stern German expression gazing out of the infant's birth-blue eyes. She called him Arthur so many times by mistake that the name stuck.

Arthur was a seldom-smiling, bright, and curious child of three when his parents placed him in the children's house, where they thought he would grow like a desert flower with the other kibbutz children. They truly believed the company of his peers was the best environment for him; he was such an odd, serious toddler. Oops! Do you feel a shudder of alarm? Did little Arthur feel a similar premonition as he clung to his mother's leg on the porch of his new home?

The revolutionary idea of the kibbutz, where socialism could thrive in its purest form, from each according to his or her ability to each according to his or her need, did not take into account that some needs are emotional and cannot be solved by committee. Nowadays socialism is a little less pure on Aron's kibbutz. Children sleep in their parents' homes and only spend a few hours a day in the children's house. This was because the mothers complained; most of the children were happy enough with the status quo.

Arthur was an exception. There is always at least one child in a class who is branded an outcast, and it is not necessarily the frail, the bespectacled, the ill-favored, or the unathletic who is selected. The distinguishing mark may be subtle; the child who draws abstract designs instead of objects may be the one to get "unhappy childhood" stamped on his or her forehead. Adults can seldom see the mark of Cain, but children always do. "Ah," they say, "you're meant to have an unhappy childhood. We'll dislike you." Manya had that stamp still clearly written on her. Emilia Larsdatter saw it, because she used to have one, and Arthur saw it, because his was concealed beneath his costume.

If Arthur had been able to escape to his mother's tender embrace after being teased, if he could have sat on his strong father's lap after being insulted, he might have been all right. But Arthur only saw his mother and father three times a day: once during afternoon break, when they were tired from work (half an hour), once in the dining hall, when he ate with them at a long crowded table (an hour and a half), and once at night, when they came in to kiss his forehead (five minutes). That left all the other hours of the day for loneliness and hurt and rejection from his peer group.

By the age of nine, Arthur was so miserable and withdrawn that his parents decided to move to Tel Aviv. Arthur adjusted better to the move than they did; the stresses of their new jobs and the loss of their old friends nibbled away at their love like so many tiny mice. Eventually the fabric ripped, and Heidi moved back to Germany, taking Arthur with her. She worked as a secretary, and Arthur had even less time with her than before, but that was all right because he was now ten and a little bit tougher and a little bit more inaccessible. He did not allow himself to miss his father. He tucked his father's letters away in a wooden box where he also kept his last baby tooth, a bullet given to him by a soldier from the kibbutz, and a fragile white length of shed snakeskin discovered under a rock. He tucked his love for his father into a mental drawer marked "Other Life." His reserve endeared him to the children in Germany, and Arthur felt that he had found a place where he belonged. More or less.

But then, when Arthur was twelve, his life changed yet again. Aron, who had been pining for Heidi back in Israel—it is always harder to be left than to leave—flew over to Germany and found his wife desperately unhappy. The two made love and the full moon dropped low in the sky and that was that, they were together again. Aron and Heidi moved back to the kibbutz and lived happily ever after. More or less. But what about Arthur? Even his own parents couldn't say that they knew him very well. When he came of age, he went to the army, which so forcibly reminded him of the children's house that he asked for, and received, a psychological release.

Ophelia was the first real friend he'd ever had, and Manya was the second.

A GIRL'S BEST FRIEND

~

Emilia Larsdatter could go for weeks without seeing a soul outside of her classes, and then panic set in. Suddenly the solitude clanged shut on her like a prison door, sending Emilia scurrying for her address book. Her manicured hand with its neat oval nails skimmed for a name, although not just any name; after a diet of bread and water, one's appetite for food shrinks, and after seclusion, one's appetite for companionship shrinks.

Six weeks into her latest bout of solitude, unable to finish the third chapter of her book, Emilia knew she wanted to see somebody. She did not, however, want to see somebody who cheated at Scrabble, or somebody whose husband was a bore, or somebody who did not enjoy foreign movies, or was selling something, or abstaining from alcohol, or about to be married and full of wedding plans. This left three names. Ring, ring, ring.

"Gosh, Emilia, how great to hear from you right before I leave for the airport. I'm about to take a year-long sabbatical in Egypt, doing research for my next book."

"This number has been disconnected. No further information is available. I repeat. This number has been disconnected."

"Hello. Yes? Oh, hi. Look, this isn't a good time to talk. Something's come up. Can I get back to you during the week? Bye."

People have their own lives and fill the empty spaces left by friends who do not call. Emilia went down her list and found that Alice was going to play bridge with a new group of friends who all cheated at games and Elizabeth's boring husband was taking scuba lessons with her every Tuesday and

Friday night, leaving them both exhausted. Sasha, who hated foreign movies, was off to attend a dog show, and was considering purchasing Colonel Furry's White Wag of Ireland. Britta, the alcohol abstainer, was dating someone she'd met at a Twelve Step meeting. Would Emilia like to come along to an alcohol-free party? Emilia politely declined. Only one name remained.

"Well, this is a nice restaurant. Oh, Emilia, I can't believe how long it's been. It's been ages, hasn't it? Why haven't we gone out together? Not that I go out much anymore," said Serena, reaching for her wine with her left hand. "You can't imagine how complicated getting married is. So much to do." Serena's left hand fluttered as she spoke.

"I can imagine. Is that your ring? It's lovely." Emilia dutifully held out her hand so that Serena could place her fingers upon it.

"Tiffany's. Simple. I like simple. You should see the other women at my office, Em. It's all one huge contest to see who's got the biggest rock. As if that counted."

"Lovely stone."

"Thanks. It's quality that counts, not size. This woman who works with me has a stone that's almost a full carat. So that's ... point one, point two ..." Serena did some quick calculations in her head. "Almost twice the size of this, say. But it's *flawed*. Anyone can see that it's flawed. When you look at it in the light, it has this strange greenish tint. I'd rather have a small stone and have it be good quality. In the end, it's the better investment."

Emilia smirked. She imagined Serena, whose sleek dark-blonde pageboy fell over one eye, hocking her ring to put food on the table, or reselling it in ten years because its market value had increased. Serena, she noted, had put on weight in the past few years; she had the affluent pouchy jowls of the not-quite-young businesswoman.

"It's still hard for me to imagine you getting married, Serena." Emilia watched as her friend gave her ring one last loving look before tucking the hand away. It was more than hard to imagine. Why, only two years ago, while recuperating from a foot operation at Mount Sinai, Serena had seduced a man visiting the patient in the next bed.

"It boggles my mind, too, but when you think about it thirty-two is certainly old enough. When Jack asked me if I wanted to move in, I said, 'I've had enough roommates to last me a lifetime.' There's a time for rent split two ways down the middle, and there's a time for engraved invitations. I also told him that if he was ever going to have kids he'd better jump on the bandwagon now, before he turned forty. How about you? What are you now, thirty-six, thirty-seven?"

"Thirty-six."

"Tick-tock goes the biological clock! Haven't you ever thought about getting married, Em? What about that writer you were seeing a while back?"

The problem with old friends is that they know the words which conjure up old demons. Serena had never been a good friend, but there had been a time ten years ago when she and Emilia had been close. Two women, roughly the same age, living nearby, struggling with careers that refused to ignite— enough common ground to lay a foundation. Serena had known where there were parties, and could be counted on to remove her shoes and dance on a table. Emilia could be counted on to glance up and remove a glass before it shattered. Drinks at a favorite bar each Friday night, war stories about men: not much in the way of intimacy, but information was exchanged. Emilia had forgotten exactly how much information. We all of us tend to forget how much we have revealed, advertently or inadvertently, to friends who are no longer close.

"You mean Saul? We broke up ages ago. That's prehistory." Emilia toyed with her wineglass, glanced at the menu, and thought about Saul, who had last left her apartment two years ago, slamming the door. He always left slamming the door. His wild mane of red hair was getting slightly grizzled, but the frenzied look in his eyes and the forceful touch of his hands remained the same. The most permanent thing about Saul, however, was the way he was always changing. Emilia could rely on hearing about his latest discovery—some new form of therapy, or religion, or woman—which he had to come tell her about in order to set the record straight between them. He wrote wonderful prose, which he ripped up, and terrible poetry, which he sent out to publishers. When he made love to Emilia, he was sometimes wonderful, which tore at her heart, and sometimes terrible, which also tore at her heart but made it easier to throw him out. Him, and the sheets. Emilia had rid herself of all the sheets he'd slept on when he left her the first time, and had continued doing so ever since. Old habits are hard to break. Emilia looked across the table at Serena and realized that her friend was talking to her.

"Oh, Em, I wish you could meet Jack," Serena was saying. "You'd like him so much, I know you would. He's very intellectual, like you. Sometimes I wonder what he's doing with someone like me, because while I consider myself bright and all, I'll be the first to admit I'd rather read something entertaining than one of those book review selections Jack's always going on about. I'm smarter about practical things. Jack's just the opposite. When I first met him he was doing really well as an actuary, he'd passed nearly all the tests and was pulling in an amazing salary, but then he got it into his mind that he had to have a purpose in life. So guess what he went and did? He entered medical school! Said that was what he always wanted. I told him he was admirable but insane. Do you know how many hours an intern works? They practically live at the hospital. Hey, maybe I should ask Jack if he has any single friends for you. Would you consider seeing someone younger, Em?"

Emilia would have snapped out a succinct rejoinder, but she saw that plump, jowly Serena was happy in the way that women were supposed to have been happy in the fifties: settled, contented, with a burbling soft mindless desire to match the world up in pairs, like Noah with his ark. Did Serena anticipate a flood? Emilia felt depressed for herself. No, she did not want a husband and children. But a lover, a companion—a diamond-ring certainty of being loved, hard and bright and virtually indestructible? Yes, that she *did* want. Someone to go home to, what Serena had. And why shouldn't she, Emilia, have what Serena had—or better? Emilia's stomach curdled with mingled feelings of superiority and envy.

"That's an idea, I suppose. But I don't count myself that desperate yet. Shall we order?"

"Good idea. Boy, I wish I had your figure, Em. I'm practically fasting these days to get into my wedding dress. Oh! Hey! Do you want to see a picture of it? I brought one along to show you."

As Serena fished around in her briefcase, Emilia suddenly felt that instead of the house salad with the Slim Pickin's packet of dressing that was in her purse, she would have escargot dripping with garlic and butter. And then the filet mignon Robespierre. And then—who knew? The sky was the limit.

"Here," said Serena, placing the photograph on the table. "Take a look at that while I go give Jack a quick call. I promised him I would."

Emilia watched Serena's broad rump as it sashayed toward the phones. It was a rump, clearly, which had been touched, would be touched, which expected to be touched as its right; it moved with the lazy assurance of a cow heading back from the milking shed. There was bread in the basket on the table, dense, crusty bread, the kind that sinks to the bottom of your stomach like a stone. Only the French could make something so hard to digest and so unreasonably delicious. Emilia broke off a piece and chewed slowly, consideringly. There were far worse things, she thought, than solitude. There were friends.

THE LOVE SONG OF MANYA MIRIAM MITTELMAN

F reshly showered, Manya lay on her bed, reading about genetic mutations for a compulsory biology course. Her hair curled damply in medusan tendrils around her face, and her thick pink terrycloth bathrobe hung loosely, baring part of one full, unbound breast. This breast and its twin were slightly swollen, as Manya's period was due in a few days.

Just another quiet Friday night.

There was a knock on the door. "Who is it?" asked Manya from her bed, expecting some hallmate who wanted to borrow her electric kettle. This time, she told herself, she would refuse to lend it unless the borrower promised to clean it out afterwards. If people wanted to save money by subsisting on packaged soup, that was fine for them, but it was not fine for her to find bits of day-old ramen noodles in her morning tea.

"It's Arthur."

"Arthur!" Manya sat up. "Wait a moment, I'm not dressed." Manya hurriedly threw on a baggy sweatshirt and a peasant skirt. She was forced to forgo undergarments, as all her bras and panties were down the hall, soaking in one of the bathroom sinks. She opened the door. "What is it? What are you doing here?"

"Oh, don't ask me what is it. I was in the neighborhood and thought I'd pay a visit. Hey, that rhymes." Arthur looked as if he had been in the neighborhood of hell. His skin was clammy, and his eyes unnaturally bright.

"Are you feeling all right, Arthur?"

"Mostly right, I would say. Aren't you going to ask me in?"

Manya dithered. She was tired and contented and focused on germ and somatic cells. After her surprise encounter with Arthur and Ophelia earlier in the day, she had decided that it would be better to prepare herself in advance before meeting them, as for any test. "Is there anything in particular ..."

"Ah, I see I am disturbing you. I'll be on my way, then." Arthur turned to leave.

Manya instantly repented her abruptness. She did not wish to seem unfriendly, and besides, how often did anyone seek out her companionship? "Arthur," she said with surrender in her voice. "It's not that I'm chasing you off. It's just that I still have studying to do."

Arthur smiled and spread his hands. "You fear I mean you harm. See, milady—no weapons. I come in peace." His eyes gleamed glassily.

"Is that one of Ophelia's quotes?"

"Are you letting me in?"

"Do I have a choice?"

They sat down, Arthur on a chair, Manya on the edge of her bed.

"Would you like some tea or coffee?" she offered.

Arthur laughed. "Absolutely no stimulants, my dear. A bad idea, caffeine. Very harsh on the system. But how about a drinky-poo? Wouldn't a drink be nice?"

"Except that I don't have any liquor."

"But I do." Arthur produced a bottle of Southern Comfort from the inside of his raincoat. He offered Manya a swig, which she refused, then drank from the bottle himself. "Did you notice how odd Ophelia was in the elevator? I think she was very odd." Arthur stood up and began pacing the length of the room. "Sometimes that girl frightens me. I think her instinct for self-preservation got washed out with her original hair color." Arthur stopped pacing and pierced Manya with an intent look. "But that is, is it not, what makes her so marvelous? She's on the knife's edge of existence. She makes the mundane seem thrilling. And have you seen her artwork? She's gifted, incredibly gifted." Arthur took up his pacing again.

"Arthur, try sitting down. What's the matter? Why are you so agitated tonight?"

Arthur bestowed a jaundiced look upon his hostess.

"Oh." Manya thought for a moment. "Maybe I will have that drink." Arthur handed her the bottle, and Manya poured a very small portion into her coffee mug.

"L'chaim." Arthur clanked her mug with the bottle. "Mind if I have a cigarette? The pause that refreshes." Arthur sat down and fumbled with his matches.

"Do you want me to do that?" Manya struck a match and held it out to him.

"My heart is pounding. Should my heart be pounding like that? Here, feel." Arthur grabbed Manya's hand and placed it on his chest.

"It's going fast, but that's normal. So is mine."

Arthur put his hand on her breast.

"Arthur!" She slapped his hand away.

"I'm not having a heart attack?" he asked piteously.

"I wouldn't think you were. Have you ever—have you done this before?"

"Been in a girl's—shall we say 'room'?" Arthur leered at her. "Only Ophelia's. And a very nice room it is. And here I am, in your room, alone with you. In some cultures, that would mean marriage or castration on the morrow. Do you know, some people think I'm gay? Doesn't bother me. People are always thinking something. *Du bist aber wunderbar* to put up with me in this terrible mood."

"You speak German?" This was proving far easier than Manya had expected. Arthur's brand of flirtation was cruder than Boris's, but it alarmed her less; she could sense no serious intent behind his verbal advances.

"Among other things. I've had a very interesting childhood. Guess where I was born."

"Germany?"

Arthur dragged on his cigarette. "*Nein*."

"Then where? France, Holland, Uruguay?"

"Israel. I am an Aryan Jew. Hitler's nightmare. What do you think about that?"

"I'm surprised." Manya wondered if he was teasing her. She took a sip from her coffee mug and realized that it was empty.

"Have some more. I'll have you know I'm the product of an extremely miserable childhood. I was everybody's nightmare. In the children's house on kibbutz, they called me 'the Nazi' because I hated sharing my toys. In Germany, the children teased me at lunchtime with 'Is it kosher? Is it kosher?' There's nothing worse than childhood. I think we should put criminals in kindergartens instead of prisons."

"I do too. Kindergartens with at least three bullies and a teacher who humiliates you by saying, 'Wake up and join us, please' and 'I think that's very meanspirited. Nobody likes a meanspirited child.'"

"Let's drink to that." They drank to that. "You're the first person I've told. Not even Ophelia knows. Ophelia hates weakness."

"You don't seem weak to me, Arthur. Quite the opposite."

As if to disprove this, Arthur began to tremble. Manya wondered if she should embrace him. She was not generally inclined to hug people, but Arthur did seem to need something of that nature. Before she had made up her mind, he stopped. "God, it's late," he said. "Too late to be late. Soon to be early. How about bringing in the early with me? Look, my lovely, I have an idea." Arthur left the room.

He returned a few minutes later with a guitar and sat beside Manya on the bed.

"Whose guitar is that?"

"I'm not entirely sure." Arthur hummed to himself as he tuned the instrument. "Do you sing?" he asked.

"Like a banshee." Manya was bemused. She was also enjoying herself. For once, she was not worried about saying the wrong thing. She was relaxed. "I'm relaxed," she said.

"I'm jamming." Arthur strummed a bit of a rock song. "Too harsh? Try this, then." A few chords shimmered briefly in the air, clues to Arthur's other life. The cocaine was zinging through his blood, lifting him up and settling him on a craggy perch, and Manya, plump little Manya, was his nest.

"That's wonderful."

"Hmm." The song woke dead nerve endings in Arthur's heart, eased a small dose of emotion into his veins—or was that simply the drug working its chemical magic? In any case, song or drug, something conjured up fields of sand and row upon row of tiny just-planted trees, and the taste of chocolate spread in the morning, and the fierce, freckled sneer of one of Arthur's childhood enemies. Spindly legs, hairless, kicking a soccer ball from Arthur's grasp. Weak tea, lukewarm, tasting of its plastic pitcher.

Manya watched Arthur's fingers. There was silence in her, deep enough that she could isolate each beat of her heart, and an awareness of her thighs pressed together. Arthur's wild sadness communicated itself to her, as such things do; it stirred an answering emotion. Here was a fellow survivor of an unhappy childhood, a kindred spirit. A fierce desire to comfort and protect Arthur rose in Manya; she was at a particularly vulnerable moment in her menstrual cycle.

Arthur put the guitar down, face up, on the floor.

"Why are you stopping? That was lovely." She felt that she was adrift in time outside of time, floating in a bubble, and all the rest of her life was outside that bubble.

Arthur sighed and looked at her. Slowly, signaling every motion, he buried his head between her breasts. For a long time he was still.

"Please don't, Arthur." But her fingers brushed his hair, and did not pull him away. What was she thinking? She barely knew herself. His nose nuzzled her through the fabric of her sweatshirt, and then his lips. What was she feeling? A delicious sweet sadness, sharp and brief as an insect bite, inseparable from pleasure. His hands, as cool as marble, caressed her, and her heavy breasts were delicate under his touch. Deftly, he sculpted her hips, her waist, her buttocks, he bestowed upon her the gift of his desire, and she could not refuse this chance to be beautiful.

Arthur's face climbed upward to her, smiled directly into her eyes. She was so nervous that she had trouble swallowing as he eased her back onto the bed so that he straddled her.

"I won't make love to you, don't worry," he said as he took off her sweatshirt. She did not think to ask what he meant. She thought he was saying that he wouldn't enter her. What he meant was, it was not love.

BEHIND DOOR NUMBER ONE
~

So you're back," said Ophelia. Her eyes were rimmed with red. She looked small and wan, a very human vampire that night.

"I'm back." Arthur stared at her. She was lying on the mattressed floor, seemingly relaxed, but a pall of misery clung to her like a cloud. The air was thick with sweet smoke, however; perhaps there was nothing more to it than that.

"And have you fleshed your will in the spoil of her honor?"

"I beg your pardon?"

"All's well that ends well. It means, have you blooded your sword?"

"Don't be vulgar, Ophelia. Do you have anything?"

Ophelia rolled over onto her stomach. "You know damn well the coke's gone. Have some grass. It'll mellow you out a bit." She reached for some papers. Suddenly she looked up, and he saw that she had been crying. "I hate you," she said brokenly.

Arthur was silent.

"I'm sorry I yelled at you before. I guess I was just coming down. Where did you go, anyway? Did you see Manya?" Pause. "Aren't you going to say anything? What is it, you don't like me when I'm not a tough little bitch?" At his continued silence, Ophelia hurled one last dart. "What do you want from me? Should I be quieter—like dear darling tubby meek mouse Manya?"

Arthur watched Ophelia warily. Then he sagged to the floor. "Please roll. I feel lousy." Arthur reached out to ruffle the hair above Ophelia's brow, and she flinched.

"Cut it out," she said. "No pity."

"Look, I only went over to Manya's because a maudlin mood had overtaken me. You would have laughed. I expended my tears on her plump bosom, and that was all."

"Do you mean it?"

Arthur nodded.

Ophelia snarled, "But it's the middle of the fucking night!"

She pounced on him, and they tumbled together. The bag of grass dropped to the floor, spilling its contents. A green bud clung to Ophelia's cheek.

"You're jealous. But that's wonderful. That's fantastic."

Ophelia stared into his eyes. Her own eyes grew wide, wider. They seemed, like a cat's eyes, to have a membrane which closed, shutterlike, over her innermost thoughts. Arthur could not tell what lay hidden behind the coke and the pot and the posturing.

"So," Ophelia said at last. "Was she any good?"

BEHIND DOOR NUMBER TWO

~

"I won't make love to you, don't worry," said the young man as he took off Manya's sweatshirt. She did not think to ask what he meant. She thought he was saying that he wouldn't enter her. What he meant was, it was not love.

Boris gasped and sat up in bed. He ran his hand over his stubbled chin and tried to figure out what was wrong. He was hung over; in a drunken desire to mark the change in his life love had wrought, he had shaved his beard off before going to sleep. There was no headache, no blurriness of vision, just a jolt of being awake and troubled. He glanced at the clock—four in the morning. In the dim illumination of the predawn sky, Boris could see the open cardboard orange juice container atop a well-stocked bookshelf, his half-eaten dinner on the round table by the window, and the empty bottle of vodka resting sideways on the chair.

Suddenly the dream came back to him.

Boris's great-great-grandfather had been called Chaim Gott, or Chaim God. The old man had been not a rabbi but a kabbalist, someone who knew secrets of mystic Jewish lore. His reputation for holiness was such that even the Christians asked him to bless their crops. The Jews listened to Chaim Gott's dreams; when the old man dreamt of fire, they buried their good copper samovars and awaited a pogrom. Chaim himself had been skeptical of his talents. "What am I," he would say, "a book that everybody can read to find out what happens next?" But when his daughter Maryasha dreamt that the mirrors in the house were covered with black cloths, Chaim settled his affairs, and died the next week.

Boris could recall this story as if he were remembering it firsthand, complete with images, odors, and sounds. Yet Boris remembered the Russia of his own childhood only dimly, and his own father not at all. Boris's mother had decided to apply for permission to join her cousins in New York immediately after her divorce from Boris's father, who had agreed to relinquish all rights to his six-year-old son. So it was possible that Boris had half-siblings, a whole other half-family in his homeland. The thought of going back for a visit had occurred to Boris, but having grown up in a community of expatriates, he suspected that the real Russia could only prove disappointing. He knew that his true homeland was the invention of nostalgia and creative remembering. His Russia was a blend of literature, poetry, music, and food, a country delineated by lavish celebrations of birthdays and bar mitzvahs. Other lands had ancient rings of stone and buttressed castles; Boris's Russia had tales of persecution and bravery. In the oral museum

Boris visited, instances of miraculous happenings and divine intervention were as common as shards of antique glass.

So as he sat there naked in bed, with one hand on his unbearded chin and the other on his suddenly roiling stomach, Boris did not try to analyze his dream. He merely attempted to recall it in full. But the images had ducked like porpoises beneath the surface of his conscious thoughts, leaving only a faint ripple to mark their passage through his brain. *Come back,* he commanded, and one lone cetacean leapt into the air: Manya, crying, fair and round and nude on her unmade bed.

Think of the things that lie buried in our brains: impressions we barely register, minutely detailed observations we clump into a vague general picture, intuitions we discount. Why, whole forests might come of the sudden insights we nip in the bud! If we only let ourselves know the half of what we know, we might all of us be prophets, or at least psychics for some popular tabloid. So perhaps there was nothing so uncanny about Boris's dream.

Or do you think that true love triggered a mystic gene in Boris's makeup, a gene inherited from Chaim Gott, blesser of crops and foreteller of disasters yet to be?

Whether Boris's dream was born of anxiety or prescience, one thing was certain. It gave him no peace. It was exactly as if he had opened a door and discovered Manya in another man's arms; possibly worse, since the door he had opened was in his own mind.

BEHIND DOOR NUMBER THREE

~~

Emotions are all a matter of interpretation. A rush of adrenaline hits the bloodstream, and up in the brain the little bureaucrats of thought hand down a decision: It's anger. No, it's love.

Manya fell in love with Arthur. Just like that. She had woken to find herself alone without explanation. Now, while she lay in bed, shivering with reaction, the central office for adrenaline interpretation delivered its verdict. *Why, I love him,* she thought. *That's why I went to bed with him.* She had made space for him in her bed, in her body; now she made a room for him in her head. He entered it in bits and pieces—the sadness in his eyes, the dexterity of his fingers on the guitar and on her flesh, a few gentle mocking phrases thrown her way. Suddenly these things were anointed with the sweet pure oil of longing, longing that having taken her, he should want her, that having left his mark upon her, he should recognize her as his.

Do you doubt this sudden love? You should. Manya should. It was not a love prompted by the discovery of another, not a love born out of the recognition that another's journey has all the charm of the foreign and all the lure of the familiar. Rather, it was a love concocted in the ramshackle laboratory of emotions, where one part sacrifice, one part shock, and a base level of low self-esteem can result in something monstrous: a self-deluding passion. Now, you may want to call this form of love infatuation, but what is infatuation if not a fancy word for a love that is ill-conceived and doomed to an early demise? By whatever name it goes, it is always recognizable, for it carries within it the tiniest germ of self-knowledge. No one is ever completely fooled by it who does not willingly collaborate in the deception.

Manya willingly collaborated. She sprayed her hair with mousse and plumped her curls with unsteady fingers; she brushed rouge on her cheeks and dressed herself in her maiden's robes, or more precisely, her maiden's sweatshirt and peasant skirt. Then she glanced at the clock—it was the unsteady hour of 1:00 a.m.—and took her coat off its hook and departed into the night.

Netted between the Grecian white pillars of the library atop the steps and the green-domed buildings beyond, the sky was a deep, bruised blue bordering on black. The slightly uneven bricks posed some difficulty for Manya's moccasin boots, so that she had to keep her head down to keep from slipping ignominiously onto her rear. She was a little frightened, both of being out in the middle of the night and of her errand. At least she was not entirely alone. In the distance, a band of hearty revelers, their shadowy forms lunging and gamboling like retrievers on a hunt, whooped loudly and then shushed themselves into muted gaiety. As the saying goes, at college each person must make his or her own choice; sacrifice sleep, study, socializing, or sustenance, for there is time enough for three but never time for four.

It seemed a century, but it had only been two weeks ago that Arthur had pointed out his room to Manya before they all left for the party. He lived on Ophelia's hall, but his room, unlike hers, was shared. Manya had caught a brief glimpse of it: an anonymous prison cell on one side, an ethnic mélange of wall hangings and prints on the other. The austere side was Arthur's. His roommate worked nights as an ambulance driver—a job Arthur had encouraged him to take.

"Arthur?" Manya knocked, then knocked again. "Arthur?" She swallowed, steeled herself, tried the door. Unlocked, it swung open, revealing dark emptiness. Relieved, then troubled, she stood a moment in thought. Manya's heart pounded through an assortment of rhythms, as if she were an electronic keyboard and someone were experimenting with different drumbeats: bossa nova, rumba, polka, waltz. Gliding into his room, Manya touched the flat, unwrinkled covers of Arthur's bed (a kibbutz child learns to make a sharp sheet corner) and slid her fingers over his books. A thought occurred; her heart dipped from waltz back to polka, from polka to the driving intensity of hard rock. Puppetlike, Manya made her way across the hall, down three doors to Ophelia's room. This time, she did not knock.

The lights were not on, and there was a dense fog of smoke, but Manya could still make out their naked forms, entwined atop the mattressed floor. They were not asleep. They did not notice her.

TO SLEEP, PERCHANCE TO DREAM

~~

Adolescence is a curious time; the body thrums with life, with hormones and lust, and the mind echoes with thoughts of death. Perhaps it is because the flip side of carnality is mortality: carnality exerts itself with such a positive force on the adolescent body that the psyche responds with an equal and opposite reaction. Or perhaps the loss of childhood reverberates through the system like the first pealing of a dire bell: Time is passing! Time is passing! Voices deepen, breasts bloom, muscles bulge and hips broaden, hair bursts like fauna in a desert flash flood, cropping up in formerly smooth hills and valleys. What else can an adolescent do but write bad poetry about decay in nature? Although for some, of course, the thoughts of death are all too appropriate. Who doesn't have a friend who died at the age of seventeen or so?

Ophelia raised her head from Arthur's shoulder. Pot and sex had eased them both into a dreamy, drifting state, not as thick as sleep, but as mindless. She lifted herself up and gazed down at her naked body—at her breasts, as flat and firm almost as a boy's, at her ribs, which appeared with each deep inhalation—running a hand over the shallow inward curve of her stomach. She glanced at Arthur, lying so near sleep that it was as if he slept. *Near sleep, near death,* she thought. Death was in the room. Death was always following her around.

"You do know," said Death, seated in an armchair which had not previously existed, "that the young who are especially obsessed with thoughts of death tend to die young." Death, Ophelia noticed, really did resemble the classic hooded figure with scythe, but was smoking a pipe and sitting with crossed legs.

"Of course I know that. Shakespeare's Ophelia and her Hamlet, James Dean, Keats, Jesus Christ, Marilyn Monroe, Dylan Thomas, Sylvia Plath. Those who are impelled to burn brightly before burning out," said Ophelia. "My heroes."

Arthur, beside her, groaned and rolled over. Though it

made no sound, her interior dialogue was loud enough to disturb him.

"Of course, of course," said Death. "And they were all impelled by premonitions of their early deaths, like you are."

"It's my fate to die young—as you should know, Death."

"I prefer to be called Dr. Death, if you don't mind. People are so familiar with me these days. 'Death' lacks a certain respect. I am the counterpoint to the whole of creation, after all, and without me existence just wouldn't have that special tang. But back to your problem, my dear. The thought had never occurred, I take it, that they, like you, might be victims of a self-fulfilling prophecy?"

Ophelia considered this. Once, when she was seventeen, she had helped bathe her grandmother. The old woman, whose cunning and spirit had always endeared her to Ophelia, had recently become senile. Ophelia had sponged the frail shoulders and breasts and gazed up at a small painting, done from a photograph, of her grandmother as a newlywed. It was not a good painting, but underneath the marcelled brown hair and blunt brows a deep, knowing gray gaze stared out from the oils. Those same eyes, now fishlike and coated with something like aspic, wobbled vacantly in their sockets, seemingly centuries distant from sight.

"Perhaps it's the fate of my choosing, my destiny of preference. To my mind, there's a fate worse than death," said Ophelia. "There's death-in-life. Zombification. Otherwise known as old age."

Death sighed. "The young always believe that by dying young they come out ahead of the game. My dear, there is no victory in choosing death rather than waiting for it to choose you—unless, of course, you believe in an afterlife. There's a popular notion that ghosts look like the bodies they wore when they died. Perhaps you think that you'll waft about in an unwrinkled soul for all eternity?"

"I, sir, am an existentialist. The hope of heaven and the wheel of reincarnation do not reassure me. If you can wrap your mind around the thought that consciousness is a constant, even if flesh is not, then good luck to you. But for all I can tell, I'm an animal, just like the other animals. It never bothers me to think that a cockroach's essential identity is clinging to the sole of my shoe, so why should it bother the universe if I'm rotting in the earth? The only way to immortality is through other people's minds."

The hooded figure pulled on his pipe. "And you want to be remembered as young and beautiful and tragic?"

"I want to be remembered. As any good artist knows, the key to creating something of lasting value is knowing when to stop creating. Too many details can end up ruining the pure line of a work, and a long life is a mass of accumulated detail, much of it extraneous and embarrassing. In addition, death at a young age is poignant. No matter how great an artist you are, there's nothing poignant about having someone stick a gloved finger up your ass when you're ninety-three and impacted."

"Hence the Doomsday Coalition rally?"

"It's not an entirely new idea, but then, there really aren't any new ideas, just new ways of doing them. I like to think that my suicide will be the pinnacle of performance art. Look how often Kennedy's assassination is replayed on television: the once and future king, killed so he shall reign forever." Ophelia smiled to herself in the dark. "I shall truly be Ophelia of the gentle madness, inspiring Hamlets and Horatios left and right."

Death tugged on his pipe. "My poor Ophelia, you are such a flirt. Do you really think to join me so soon? I'll wager you won't. My old nemesis Life has a surprise in store for you."

"We'll just see about that, Dr. Death!" Tired of the game, she banished the Grim Reaper to the recesses of her imagination. Then she turned to Arthur. "I'm going to burn in your memory," she whispered. "You'll be my high priest when I'm gone."

Groaning, Arthur turned over. It was not a good night.

LADY IN AN IVORY TOWER

L ove, that old alloy of precious metal and some less pure, is not invulnerable to sudden blasts of extreme force. Love tempered by time can withstand a great many shocks, but Manya's love had been a flimsy thing, made in haste to fit the occasion. It broke on impact.

Once upon a time there was a plump college freshman who loved nineteenth-century English novels and was a virgin until she got involved with a charming, dissolute young man. Not Manya and Arthur. Manya's mother, Sophie, and Manya's father, Huxley. Huxley had been kicked out of his first college, a Catholic school, for improprieties committed with a professor's wife. Huxley, it seemed, was looking for a warm, maternal presence. He found it in Sophie. Sophie and Huxley got married, and Sophie quit school so that she could support her husband. Huxley dissected rats while Sophie typed, and they were both pretty much content with the way things were—Sophie doing all the housework and bringing in all the money, Huxley conducting studies in rodent aggression and flirting with his professors' wives—until Sophie got pregnant.

Now, wasn't Manya lucky?

Unfortunately, Manya didn't feel lucky. She felt that she'd loaned out her body as casually as her electric kettle and it had been returned to her soiled and used, without so much as a thank you. How could she have been so smart about Boris and so stupid about Arthur? And, she thought, it was not a mistake that could be retracted; words sometimes are forgotten, but what has been seen and felt and touched is indelibly printed on the senses. Manya burned with humiliation, too innocent to know that she was wrong, for it is words which are indelible and the senses which have a short memory.

To think she had given him access to her innermost self, to the secrets of her flesh! But he had only nibbled at her innermost self as if it were an appetizer, and then gone back to Ophelia for dinner. Or was that dessert, or just deserts? Manya, who had been picking at her feet in distress, tore her toenail loose from its bed of cuticle.

Even a flimsy love, hastily made and quickly broken, requires a fair amount of emotional cleaning up afterwards. Manya, viewing the state of her psyche, knew that a strong cleanser was required. Rage. Not at Arthur, mind you. At herself. Or, to be more specific, at her flesh.

Flesh. Nasty, pustulant, solid and sullied flesh, sweating and belching and farting and reeking flesh, salivating, secreting, and excreting all manner of substances, swelling and bleeding, sprouting wanton hairs and wayward warts, graceless, mindless, base and feculent, exuding ooze. Oh, the expense of spirit in a waste of shame! The spirit got a terrible beating as it was, thought Manya, without having to be dragged about by the flesh and wastefully expended. How ignoble it all was. The life of the mind, the yearnings of the heart, the hope of the spirit, were one and all subjugated to the crass demands of the flesh. If only the flesh weren't so closely connected with the spirit! The spirit had such wonderful moments of illumination, and all the flesh ever did was intrude and say, "We're hungry now. We have to pee now. We're horny now." Or worst of all, the flesh nudged the spirit and whispered mockingly, "When I go, I'm taking you with me." And not content with all of this, the flesh insisted on impinging itself on the spirit in more subtle ways, so that its carnal pleasures moved the spirit to bliss and its mortal pains plunged the spirit into a slough of despond. *If not for you,* she thought, pinching her flesh, *I would have been just fine tonight.*

Now Manya knew what heartache was—it was the birth pang of wisdom. But what was the lesson in all this?

The lesson, clearly, was to restrain herself in a mental chastity belt. She would guard herself well. She would retrieve what she could of her self-respect and build a wall around it. A wall and a moat. She would be a lady in an ivory tower, and whosoever battered at her gates would batter in vain.

There were ways she knew to appease the flesh and mortify it after; ways which required that she leave the room but not the fortress of her solitude.

It seemed colder outside now than it had been half an hour ago, and Manya encountered no students as she walked toward Broadway. Her heart beat rapidly, from fear this time, not from excitement. She had never ventured the streets at this hour before. *I'm being brave,* she thought. *Intrepid.* She knew what she needed—to feel better, now, immediately—and it was worth the danger. By the time Manya reached the twenty-four-hour deli, her fear had passed, replaced by relief and gratitude.

On the way back, Manya stuffed a Devil Dog into her mouth and ate it in five bites, then unwrapped a candy bar and ate that in three. She unlocked her door with one hand, slammed it shut behind her with a kick, sat down on the dingy carpet, and continued eating—peanut butter scooped from the jar, bites of frozen waffle—while taking off her coat and shoes. She was feeling better, and paused long enough to take the tabloid she'd bought out of the bag. CHER PREGNANT AGAIN! blared the headline. A smear of peanut butter from Manya's fingers marred Cher's sinuous midriff. The time was 1:45 a.m.

Half an hour later, Manya had eaten the entire contents of the bag, which included:

1 large apple cheese strudel
10 mini pizzas
1 small jar peanut butter
1 package frozen Belgian waffles
1 pint chocolate-chocolate-chip ice cream
12 ounces nacho cheese chips

The total caloric content was roughly nine thousand one hundred and seventy-five. Of course, Manya had also eaten the Devil Dog (two to three hundred calories) and the candy bar (two hundred and fifty calories). In addition, she had eaten a tuna salad platter for lunch (four hundred calories) and had breakfasted meagerly on orange juice and coffee with skim milk (one hundred to one hundred and fifty calories).

Manya's combined intake for the day (counting this as one

day, even though it was well past midnight) was over ten thousand calories. The total number of calories a woman her age and size should consume on an average day, allowing for a moderate level of exercise, is two thousand two hundred or so—maximum. A woman answering to Manya's profile eating ten thousand calories a day could easily expect to become obese within, shall we say, one month.

Do you know how to consume over ten thousand calories in a day and still manage not to gain weight? Manya knew.

Ducking into the communal bathroom, which was empty, Manya locked herself into the far stall. Then she knelt down, lifted the toilet seat, and sighed deeply. There were no rings on her right hand, but a careful observer might have noticed a thin scar on the back of her reddened first knuckle. This finger, pushed past the epiglottis, tickling the back of the throat, induces reverse peristalsis in humans. Not in cows, however; cows cannot regurgitate their food, and must die if poisoned, or grow fat if greedy. Dogs will eat grass to promote vomiting if they feel the need; cats, especially those prone to hairballs, seem to vomit almost at will.

Manya vomited silently and in stages, the last food she had eaten reappearing first. She paused whenever a spontaneous retching noise escaped her, to insure that she would not be discovered. The final rush of bitter brown liquid, sour and sharp with a large quantity of gastrointestinal acid, heralded the end of the act.

Binge and purge. A simple formula, followed by more young women than we know or care to guess. The plumbing of entire universities has been fouled by the secretions of these young women's stomachs; stomach acid is powerful stuff. Binge and purge. Manya flushed the toilet, wadded up toilet paper and cleaned the rim of the bowl, and flushed again. She emerged cautiously from the stall, walked to the sinks, and washed her face and hands. Her nose was running, her ears rang slightly, and her eyes were red and brightened by tears. Manya brushed her teeth with her finger, having forgotten her toothbrush. There was toothpaste on the sink, left by some other student. On purpose? For what purpose? Manya did not know.

Bulimia is a solitary sport.

THE ALLURE
OF UNAVAILABILITY
~~

The next day, at Zaftigue, Boris's fears were confirmed. He was too old a hand at mornings-after not to recognize the telltale signs; Manya's pallor, her splotchy chin and forehead, the oily lankness of her hair, all spoke eloquently of a night begun in passion and ended in regret. She even moved differently, with a languor tinged with sadness, just this side of lethargy. Was he to blame? Had his declaration of love, which had pushed her away from him, sent her toppling like a domino into some stranger's concupiscent custody?

"These goods are all damaged, Boris. Aren't you going to complain about it?"

Boris, aghast, took a moment to respond. Every single thing Manya said seemed to have a second and unsavory meaning. She appeared to be handling this far better than he, speaking of practical matters with a composure that he could admire but not emulate. Boris wanted nothing more than to comfort the erring object of his affections, to be her friend once more, to offer a shoulder on which her tears could fall, to protect her and be the fortress that stood between her and all alien invaders.

The problem was, Manya didn't seem to need comforting; Boris could see she had built her own defenses. It made him miserable. It made him love her all the more. She had all her old charm, and the added allure of unavailability.

There is nothing like the allure of unavailability. It is the most potent aphrodisiac known to mankind—or womankind, for that matter. Listen up, you who would be adored! The slight turning away of a face hides many flaws, and the terse forming of the word "no" conceals much shallowness. The faraway look in a lover's eyes, the hint of infidelity imagined or real, adds more mystery than all of Salome's veils and Mata Hari's aliases.

Boris stroked his clean-shaven chin, and was embarrassed by its nakedness. Manya moved about, rustling clothes, then sat on a stool by the desk. Growing desperate to evoke some response from her, Boris resorted to drawing attention to what he was beginning to think of as his deformity.

"Manya. *Dyevotchka.* Have you not yet noticed that my beard is gone?"

"It looks good. It looks really good. It makes you look younger." Manya bit her finger, tearing at the cuticle.

"Then why did you not say something before? You could have said, 'Boris, you are so handsome that your razor deserves to be put in a museum, with da Vinci's paintbrushes and Michelangelo's chisel.'" Standing propped against the surly, raincoated 1940s mannequin, Boris penciled off a figure in the accounts book.

"I don't know. I guess because when I get a new haircut, I hate it when people compliment me. I never know whether they're telling the truth." Manya combed her fingers through her hair. She was exhausted. Sleep had eluded her for a very long while, staved off by the weight of her depression, a depression like none she had ever known, a huge black bird of a feeling squatting on her belly. Morning had not banished the scavenger emotion; it descended before she had even opened her eyes, cawing, "Wake up! Wake up! Time to suffer!"

"Sometimes, Manya, people do tell the truth." Boris put the accounts book down.

"This is true. And sometimes they don't. And how the hell can you tell the difference? Said the man from Thebes, 'There's one thing you can count on; all the men from Thebes lie.'"

Boris looked mystified. He'd never heard Manya curse before.

"Pay no attention to my babbling. Hey, it's almost lunchtime. Should I run out to the store?" What Manya really wanted was to have no one look at her, no one talk to her, no one touch her. She thought she would like to be a Muslim woman so she could wrap her head in a thick black veil and walk with eyes downcast, unassailable. She could be happy living in purdah. It sounded like a village in the mountains where you might rent a country cottage.

Boris realized that he had better keep the conversation light. "It might rain. I wouldn't want you to get wet."

"There's not a cloud in the sky, Boris."

"You can never predict when it might suddenly rain at this time of year."

"Then I'll get to work reorganizing the shelves."

"But if you did get wet, you could always come back here and dry off," said Boris meaningfully. His mouth, suddenly disconnected from his brain, seemed to have its own agenda.

"Why don't you tell me what needs doing first, and I'll start."

"Sometimes it's hard to know what to do," said Boris, "to impose order when you've made a mess of things. The thing not to do is to get overwhelmed. There's always a way to set things to rights."

"Right. I'll start on the sweaters." Manya took an armful of rumpled sweaters from the dressing room and began to fold.

"Good. And remember, I'm here if you need me."

Manya sighed. Then she looked up from the sweaters. "Boris, I'm not obtuse, you know. I do know what you're trying to tell me."

"That's a relief," said Boris, "since I'm not sure myself."

This last remark effectively killed the conversation. As the hours went by, Boris and Manya buried what was left of the taboo subject under layers of politeness.

Five hours later, on her way back from Zaftigue, Manya felt the raven of depression sink its talons into her shoulder.

To binge or not to binge? That was not the question. The question, Manya thought, was whether to plunge into Zabar's, still two blocks away, and brave the throngs of delicatessen-mad shoppers, or whether to settle for the less exciting fare to be had at a store closer to home. It was a warm mid-October evening. Manya opted for Zabar's.

Ah, Zabar's! A binger's paradise and a loner's purgatory. Counter after counter of food: glassy-eyed chubs, herring salads, roast beefs that blushed at their own good looks; knishes stuffed with cheddar, spinach, sweet potato;

rugelach, massive tins of Italian almond cookies, chocolate-dipped orange peel, chocolate-dipped strawberries, dark chocolate, milk chocolate, toffee crunches; goat's cheese, sheep's cheese, spicy sausages; and people, people, shoving and waving and yelling to each other, people dressed in massive raccoon coats, in tattered denim, in pastel polyester. There were even announcements over the loudspeaker, as in an airport: "Attention, shoppers, attention, shoppers. There is a special on whitefish salad today, at the fish counter." Stampede! A herd of well-heeled buffalo, trampling the Great Plains underfoot! The shoppers, nothing if not attentive, made their way to the fish counter, pulling numbers from the ticket machine with the avidity of gamblers. Regarding the scene somewhat balefully were the white-aproned men who doled out delicacies with thick-fingered hands and moved with steady purposefulness.

"May I help you, miss?"

Manya picked with the care of an experienced binger. Meat, which the body digests at its leisure, is a chokingly unpleasant affair to throw up. Hard cheese hardens still more. Let it be soft and spongy and creamy, and it will return soft and spongy and creamy. Let it be tough to break down, and what your high school science teacher taught you will be proven: the hydrochloric acid your stomach produces is strong, strong stuff. How can anyone about to do something so distasteful be so logical? Like a runner who knows that his muscles will ache, like a warrior anticipating the blow of the enemy's sword upon his shield, Manya did not flinch from the knowledge of what would follow. She was entering the land of pain, where she had been an unwilling visitor four years ago.

A VERY BRIEF CHAPTER
MARKING THE PASSAGE OF TIME
~~

As October progressed, the leaves of Columbia's trees turned brown and dropped without pausing for colorful transition. The weather remained fairly warm and pleasant during the day, and the nights grew colder. Manya withdrew into her studies, accompanied everywhere by her faithful pet, the black bird of unhappiness. She avoided both Arthur and Ophelia as much as possible, for the merest glimpse of their blond heads caused the raven to nibble jealously at her eyeballs.

Boris, who Manya mistakenly thought had gotten over her, longed for her from afar for most of the week, and then from anear for the two days when she worked at Zaftigue. He did not, however, completely stop dating other women.

Vanessa spent hours reminiscing about her brief affair with Boris, and sometimes walked by Zaftigue, but never actually went inside.

Ophelia, giddy as a bride, was preparing for her special day—Doomsday, that is. She had not realized that it would be so unromantic, but even the necessity of making phone calls and writing letters and researching various organizations did not deter her. So busy was she, in fact, with making her plans that she did not notice the plans life was making for her.

Arthur trundled along after Ophelia, hitched, as it were, to her wagon, but making sardonic comments along the way.

And as for Emilia, she was preparing midterms as the month drew to its close, and beginning to wonder when Saul was coming back into her life.

THE MINEFIELD OF LOVE
~

Emilia had lived for so many years on the precarious border of an undead relationship that she sometimes forgot that before the great shift, things had been different. There had been a time—so long ago and far away, so shrouded in the mists of memory that it had attained mythic proportions—when she and Saul had been happily in love. His red hair had not looked then like the electric mane of a crazed lion, his eyes had not burned with a fierce glint, and his ideas for personal redemption had been only lightly touched with madness. Those were the days when Saul and Emilia walked hand in hand through the East Village, eating cheap eggplant curries in tiny Indian restaurants, pressing up against each other in dark corners, his hand under her skirt, her hand cradling his face. She was going to be a brilliant writer of feminist philosophy; he was going to rewrite the Bible as an epic poem. Then they had their first real argument.

"You're the brain and I'm the heart," he said. "One flesh in two."

"I have a heart of my own," she replied. "You have your own brain."

"You're too literal. You destroy the meaning behind the meaning. You use words as weapons, to tear at the soul of things."

"You just want me to say exactly what you want me to say. I think my own way. If you want to have a relationship, you have to allow for differences."

"This isn't working. What you call differences I call shit. It's all shit, Emilia. Big, stinking, smelly dark feces. I want to cut through the shit! I want communion, I want clarity, I want communication!"

"What are you talking about?"

"I need to go out. I need time to walk and think. This is not how I expected things to work out between us."

"But where are you going, Saul? I thought things were fine between us. Things were fine a minute ago."

"Then sort things out. I don't have the patience for this kind of crap from you, Emilia."

Eventually she realized that one of them was crazy. For a year and a half, she assumed it was she who was causing the fights. For six months, she thought it was both of them. For one hour, she considered aloud that it might be Saul—and then he left, storming out the door in a fury.

He always returned. For an hour, for a weekend, for a month. To tell her he had changed, that he needed her, didn't need her, to make love to her and cause a little pain. They walked a minefield of love for a brief while, stepping delicately around the submerged explosives—her way of thinking about commitment, his drinking, her father, his spending—until, out of clumsiness or to break the unbearable tension, one of them picked a bomb to tread on and blew the affair up again.

More than enough time had passed. Saul was overdue. Emilia stared at the phone and willed it to ring.

Finally, it did. Not knowing how she knew, Emilia heard her lover's strident summons in the ringing. The alarum had sounded. Emilia armed her spirit and answered.

"Hello?"

"Hello, Emilia."

"Saul! My God, I was just thinking about you."

"I'm in the States for a little while. I have something monumental to tell you."

"Don't you always? Well, come on by." Emilia thought guiltily of the papers she had not graded and the exams she hadn't finished writing. But she could always do that later on in the evening—or early in the morning, if it came to that. Saul was her knight in tarnished armor, her ill-fated soldier of fortune back from the wars, and Emilia was fully prepared to be conquered. At least for a time.

But this time, when Saul arrived, he had a new weapon. He aimed it at Emilia and fired immediately, before she had a chance to prepare herself for the attack.

"Emilia."

"Saul!" She embraced him. Then she noticed the young woman by his side. The very young woman.

"Hello," said Emilia slowly, struck by the horrendous thought that this was his daughter, that Saul had gotten some woman pregnant sixteen years ago and never told her.

"Emilia, meet Cecile." Saul's arm, which Emilia now saw was around the young woman's shoulders, tightened affectionately. "My wife."

"Wife!" said Emilia. "Wife!" Her mouth gaped.

"Emilia," said Cecile, giving the name its precise and

melodious French pronunciation. "It is lovely to meet you at long last."

"How long can it have been?" snapped Emilia, turning to Saul. "Since last month, when she started menstruating?"

Cecile laughed murmuringly, deep in her throat. "I am not disappointed, Emilia. Saul told me about your wits."

"Having lost all his own, I presume." Emilia flung the door open. "Do come in," she said.

"Emilia," said Saul warningly, but Cecile had already sailed ahead into the apartment. Emilia realized that Cecile was not quite as young as she had first assumed; that is to say, she was in her twenties, not her teens. She wore her extreme youth with extreme poise. She was bonelessly slender, with a dark head of hair like the pelt of a seal. Her jacket was made of fine black leather. Her lips were thin and loveless. She was French.

"So," said Emilia when they were all seated in the living room and equipped with cigarettes and cups of coffee, "when did all this happen?" Emilia smiled, showing teeth.

"Yesterday." Saul, bearlike, clapped a hand around his young bride's shoulders. He looked vigorous and happy. "Now I'm taking Cecile to the East Village. She's never been there before."

"You got married yesterday? When did you meet? Last week?"

"We met a year ago, in France. I cannot marry Saul there, you see, because I am Catholic, and I have already married once in the church." Cecile gave a Gallic shrug of acceptance.

"You've already been married once before? My, my. When did you find the time? No, don't answer that, my dear. I'm sure you're very efficient. When are you two lovebirds going back? Are you going back?"

"We will go back to France next week to tell my parents

about the baby," said Cecile. She nodded her head as if acknowledging the perfect aim of her thrust, a tender regard for the victim about to fall.

Emilia could not remember the end of the conversation. She did recall the impulse, barely controlled, to do violence; but that might have come after, when she was alone again, hunched over the refrigerator, searching for food.

DISCUSSING LITERATURE,
BOOK UNREAD
~

Have you ever heard of Elizabeth Arkoway's *Flesh of Frailty?* Nobody had, it seemed, except for Emilia Larsdatter. The book was listed as out of print at the Columbia bookstore, out of circulation at the Barnard bookstore, and out of existence at three haughty secondhand bookstores in the Village. There was a rumor that it was hidden in the stacks of one of the Columbia libraries, possibly in the reference room, but the computers spat out "Arkoway" and "Flesh of," though they finally produced three poets named "Arkaway," "Ark O'Way," and "Archowae." Actually, only one student—a horn-rimmed, weak-chinned young woman who seemed to be passing from youth to middle age faster than most people pass driving exams—had searched in all these places, but the rest of the class nodded knowingly as if they, too, had been on a quest for this elusive grail.

"Well, this is most discouraging," said Emilia. "Another example of how the canon of accepted great literature determines what we read. Can you imagine Henry James's novels being out of print? Tolstoy's?"

The class murmured no, of course not, unthinkable.

"Women writers of the past are not taught, are not published, are not read. It's as simple as that. And I suppose all of you think that if Elizabeth Arkoway were really as great as all that you'd have heard of her, she'd be on the shelves, the really good writers always surface in time."

An outrage, the class muttered obediently, how we always assumed that.

"It's not true that greatness is always recognized! I mean, some say that *Flesh of Frailty* is hugely flawed, and not the best example of psychosexual dynamics because of its author's lapses into long descriptive passages about Greece lifted from a popular travelogue of the day. But isn't *Crime and Punishment* flawed? How about that ending? That really sucked, didn't it?"

Polite titters followed this remark, but there were also some restive movements from the back of the room. There was a slightly hysterical edge, growing more pronounced by the moment, in Emilia's voice. Her lecture was almost, it seemed, a tirade; and a few students could not help but notice the unruly way their professor's hair was pinned, and that her crisp blue skirt seemed to strain over her bulging stomach.

Emilia sat on her desk, slumping her shoulders. She removed her spectacles and pressed her fingers to the bridge of her nose. "Elizabeth Arkoway was an unmarried spinster, grossly overweight, who refused to wear corsets," she announced.

Ophelia was so struck by Larsdatter's behavior that she scribbled a note and passed it to Manya.

Manya crumpled the paper without reading it. Then, overcome with curiosity, she uncrumpled it and read: "The lady doth protest too much, methinks. Wonder what secrets this performance might reveal." It was the first communication between them since that Friday night, almost two weeks ago.

"Other women of her time wore corsets straight through pregnancy," Emilia snarled. "Through pregnancy! Can you imagine? Just to keep their figures slim."

"Professor," said the horn-rimmed young woman who had searched for the book, "is this biographical information truly relevant to our discussion?"

"Seeing as none of you have read the text," Emilia parried, "I'm not left with too many alternatives, now, am I?"

"We could continue our discussion of last week's novel."

"We could. We could just throw Elizabeth Arkoway out the window, forget about her and her life, and concentrate on those novels and authors whom the big guns have deemed it permissible to read." Emilia's face was taut with restrained fury. "That's where I'm going, you know. Out the window."

"Excuse me?" The young woman smiled a supercilious smile.

"Not literally, Ms. Kornbluth, not literally. What are you, anyway, nineteen? Twenty? Twenty-one?"

"I fail to see ..."

"You'll be the white-hot light of academia, I suppose? Of course you will. God bless twenty-one! The gods smile on twenty-one! Or perhaps you think you have a novel in you?"

"I see no reason for you to attack me." Ms. Kornbluth folded her hands on her desk, chastised back into good grade school behavior.

"You'll find, my dear, that this attack will smart less than the slow encroachment of reality. Wait a few years. We can't all be Colette, we can't all be Simone de Beauvoir, but does that mean we should just be shoved aside and forgotten?"

Manya looked at Emilia and recognized the nature of her pain. Professor Larsdatter, elegant and sharp, had been rejected. Manya felt a sudden rush of warmth for Emilia, and a stab of hatred for the Ophelias and Arthurs of this world, for the Sally Shickelgrubers and Adam Mandrakes. She raised her hand.

"Ms. Mittelman. You have a question?"

"Assuming that certain novels by women have survived, while others like *Flesh of Frailty* have been shunted aside, is there some subject matter that's more—I mean, putting aside the question of how good a writer Elizabeth Arkoway was, was there something about the subject matter that made the book less acceptable? Like romance novels. No one but women reads them. Maybe this was a book that only women would read?"

"Ms. Mittelman," said Emilia with surprise. "What an intelligent question."

Ophelia whispered, "Good going!"

Manya ignored her and listened as Professor Larsdatter turned her full attention to answering with respect, and even—hallelujah—admiration.

OFFICE HOURS

~

After class, Emilia went to her office in Hamilton Hall. It was a small office stuffed with a large dining room table, a thick rubber plant which had been lingering on the verge of death for months, two typewriters, five file cabinets, two bookcases, and Herman Finder, an associate professor of English. Of all these things, Emilia resented Herman most, the file cabinets next—for three of them were filled with applications and belonged to another department—and the rubber plant last, for she wanted to throw it out, and could not bring herself to do so before it was properly dead.

Emilia sat down at her side of the dining room table and stared at the typewriter. She glanced up at the photograph of Colette—hers, not Herman's—and then at the poster of a French garden shot in soft focus—Herman's, not hers. Was it too early for a drink? She looked at her watch. It was even too early for lunch.

There was a knock at the door. "Professor Larsdatter?" A pause, then again: "Professor? Are you there?"

"Come in." Emilia adjusted her skirt, which was cutting into her waist.

Ophelia entered the room as if a gust of pagan Halloween air had blown her there. She had lost weight recently, and one slim shoulder, bony as a kneecap, was exposed by a loose orange sweatshirt. Skull-and-crossbones earrings dangled from her ears.

"Ms. Saunders. How may I help you?" Emilia removed her glasses, ostensibly in order to clean the lenses on the edge of her skirt. In reality, she was trying to combat a headache that was rapidly turning vicious.

"It's a little complicated," said Ophelia.

"Not another tale of woe. Unless you have a note from the family undertaker or you want to take the exam, the paper's still due on Friday."

"It's not about the paper. It's about the Doomsday Coalition."

"I am not religious, and at the advanced age of thirty-six, I do not care to suddenly become religious. Try your fellow adolescents, if you must."

"It's not a religion. It's a coalition."

Emilia reached for a pile of papers and shuffled them. "I'm not interested in campus politics. The only politics that interest me are those of gender."

"This is above the level of most campus politics," Ophelia hastened to say. "This involves students and faculty from many different positions on the political and academic spectrum. We're attempting to reach feminists, environmentalists, anarchists, everybody. We're trying to create dialogue. We're trying to make everyone realize that we're all in this together." Ophelia covered her lips with one finger, as if forcing herself to pause and wait for a reply. Actually, she had run out of words. Professor Larsdatter's dry dismissal was making Ophelia inarticulate. She should have prepared better; charismatic people always overestimate their ability to improvise under stress.

"It sounds like chaos." Emilia bent her head to the sheaf of papers.

"Doesn't it? I suppose that's the danger of it. But we're hoping for something better."

"Hope, Ms. Saunders, is pretty far down on my list of priorities. I leave hope to those who wish to concern themselves with religion and politics."

"Forgive my saying so, but there might be a practical reason for you to get involved. We need strong speakers, and you need a wider forum for your ideas. Wouldn't it be great if you could talk about *Flesh of Frailty* to the freshmen and jocks and—and even the press? People who ordinarily wouldn't take your course. Think of the publicity! Think of tenure," Ophelia added craftily.

"How many ways must you be told, Ms. Saunders? I am not interested." *Or capable of the effort.* "I applaud your ambition, if not your grasp of what can be realistically achieved."

"Reality," said Ophelia, rallying herself, "is what we make it. Or do we just let others make it for us?"

Emilia stood up and opened the door. "Now," said Emilia, "if you have concluded your speech ..."

"Please do think it over," said Ophelia, with a trifle too much assurance.

"I suggest you think over your paper, due next Friday. If you find the time, with all your pamphleteering."

Alone, Emilia breathed a sigh of relief. Then she bent her head and wept.

"Oh, my," said Herman Finder, opening the door, his balding young countenance as unprepared as an egg for what he was seeing.

TRANSCENDENTAL SEX MEN

~

There are men who are, as Lady Caroline Lamb said of Lord Byron, mad, bad, and dangerous to know. They make love with a ferocity that melts the bones, but they do not make peace. They are the Transcendental Sex Men, and almost every woman meets one in her life. He is the man who dissolves her inhibitions, the man whose desire lifts her to the ranks of Guinevere and Cleopatra, the man who burns more brightly in her memory than many better loves. This man will tell you that he never knowingly misleads his women but can hardly prevent them from misleading themselves. "Women believe what they want to believe," is how he puts it. No wonder, then, that he leaves a trail of angry ex-lovers behind him. The cry of the abandoned is invariably the same: "You said you loved me! How could you just stop loving me when I haven't stopped loving you?" The reply is as unsatisfying as it is inarguable: "I did love you when I said that, but people change."

Now, one woman's Transcendental Sex Man (let's call him T.S.M.) may be another woman's cold plate of spinach, or even her husband. The man who is mad, bad, and dangerous for Katie to know may be good, kind, and a reasonable prospect for Sue. He may even make Sue sing between the sheets, but he won't make her scream. No woman can have her T.S.M. and keep him, too; the man who incinerates your toes with passion will not take your trash out to the incinerator.

Except in historical romances, or, as they are commonly called, bodice rippers. In these novels, the pirate or cowboy or outlaw or lord or mercenary is able to straddle an apparent

contradiction as easily as he straddles his horse and the heroine. For although the hero (let's call him Dirk) seems as brood-
ingly mysterious as a cougar, he is also as domesticated as a
neutered tomcat. Dirk is passionate, ready and willing to have
the heroine before, after, and during each meal, but he is also
ready and willing to cook the meal and clean up afterwards.

The reason this is possible in romance novels and not in
real life is that transcendental sex requires an obstacle, and
the obstacles found in genre fiction are not the same as those
found in life: alcohol or drug dependency, children from a former marriage, an ex-spouse, a wandering eye, work pressures,
illness, an inability to empathize, a deficiency of some basic
emotion. The obstacles Dirk and his lady fair face are the kind
of obstacles which add a bit of spice: a quest, a need for
vengeance, a case of mistaken identity, a case of mistaken cul-
pability, an attack from a wild marauding band.

This is why no woman is happily partnered to her T.S.M.
There are just too few quests and marauding bands about
these days.

BODICE RIPPERS

~

Vanessa was having a great deal of difficulty getting over
Boris. Perhaps it was her job; she was an editor at LoveLorn
romances, for their Regency line of novels. All day long
Vanessa read about eighteen-year-olds whose impish flouting
of convention ("I shall not perform my needlepoint, Mama!")

led them straight into the arms of dashing rakes ("You have heard rumors, Minerva, of my way with the fair sex—but there is no education like one obtained firsthand!").

Once, these books had been her escape. Now, even her fantasies of romance depressed her. I could change jobs, Vanessa thought, sitting at her desk and fingering an unsolicited manuscript. Nonfiction? Children's books? Vanessa sighed. It was almost time to go home anyway. She opened up her purse and looked for a compact. In the small mirror, she peered at her face. For years she had looked the same—hennaed hair, slight overbite, large nose, and an expression of such heedless, intrusive good nature that she seemed, metaphorically speaking, to have the hide of a rhinoceros. That was the old Vanessa, who could swallow insults as dogs swallow detritus from the street, without visible ill effect. But these days, although she was not yet thirty, she saw that something was happening to her cheeks and eyebrows. Her face was entering a new stage of life, was shifting in subtle ways. Her face was like a clock, seemingly motionless until, with a faint click, it inched itself into a different position.

"I'm never going to get married," she told her face. It told her she was probably right. "I'm never going to get married, and I'm never going to be really loved." Her face did not contradict her.

Vanessa left her office building and walked to the subway. She descended into the dank medieval depths, where urine splattered the floor and rats crawled boldly underfoot, where the ragged denizens of the caverns sat huddled here and there, largely ignored by the white-turbaned perfume vendors and the crowds. Vanessa, in her smart business suit and high heels, thought that London right before the plague could not have been more gruesome. She looked around her. The affluent merchants and the diseased lepers. The mummies and the skeletons. The mummies and the skeletons? Suddenly Vanessa realized that strange as most subway riders were, they were not usually this strange. It was Halloween. As a young child, she had loved Halloween, loved dressing up as a princess or a fairy and collecting chocolates from strangers. Out of the blue, Vanessa decided to take the train to the Village, to see the Halloween parade.

MARAUDING BANDS

~

The Halloween parade in Greenwich Village is a sight which must be seen to be believed. The most extravagant costumes imaginable are worn by the most extravagant people, and the night is filled with the hoots and hollers of pagan revelry.

"Isn't this superb?" asked Herman Finder. "Doesn't this cheer you right up?" A zombie, brushing past, spilled beer on Herman's shoulder.

"Oh, Herman, it's kind of you," said Emilia, "but it's a bit too much for me. There're so many people." After Herman found her crying in their office, he had insisted on trying to cheer her up. Now they were crammed up against a store wall, and regret was far too mild a word to describe what Emilia was feeling.

"Oh, don't go yet," said Herman earnestly. He was one of those people who have made a bargain with the devil of dissertations; Herman had completed his Ph.D. at the age of twenty-five and had published his thesis at the age of twenty-six, but now he was twenty-seven and still a virgin. "When I saw you crying, I knew this was just what you needed. Emilia, I have to tell you something, something I guess you already know, but I have to tell you how I feel about ..."

At this most inopportune of moments, a band of demons rushed by, crashing into Herman and carrying him along in their wake.

The band of demons also crashed into Emilia, but before she could be carried off someone grasped her and held her steady.

"Are you all right?" Vanessa brushed Emilia off. "What a zoo, huh?"

"I just want to get out of here," said Emilia.

"Me too. Let's stick together." Vanessa smiled.

The two women, like survivors of a war, braved the ravening crowds, walking what seemed like endless miles until they reached streets that were dark and silent. By this time, they felt like old friends, and Vanessa was telling Emilia about what she called her "Russian affair."

"There was this incredible expression of shock and awe on his face, as if an angel had just whispered in his ear. He said, 'I'm in love.' I went incredibly still, the whole room seemed to freeze in time, and then he added, very matter-of-factly, that he was not in love with me."

Emilia did not know what to say, so she squeezed Vanessa's hand.

"The thing is, it hardly seems worth all the grief I've spent on it. I've wasted weeks thinking about something that lasted forty-eight hours from start to finish. Oh, men, men, men. Maybe it's because I spend all day reading about men—heroic, romantic, passionate men—and I think there's not a man alive who would read even one book about nothing but romance. Most of the women I know have read thousands. It's ironic, when you think about it—a whole genre about relationships between men and women, read exclusively by women."

"Yes, that's true, and ..." Emilia stopped walking. "Oh, to hell with it. I was about to say something about irony, but I'm sick to death of irony. Irony's epidemic these days. In academic circles, it's fashionable to say, 'Oh, I ceased being a naïve reader eons ago,' in a tone of deep regret. 'It's one of the unfortunate side effects of making books your life,' they say, like a bunch of old whores discussing sex." Emilia turned to Vanessa with a rueful smile. "Romance novels are probably the only fiction that's uninfected by irony. I suppose the genre's immune by nature—or designed to shut down all the reader's critical faculties. Perhaps the constraints of the form demand naïveté."

Vanessa laughed. "You mean you read them too? I would've thought you'd despise them, being a professor of feminist lit."

Emilia blushed guiltily.

Vanessa laughed even harder. She looked, in that moment, flushed and attractive. She looked much as she had in the Russian restaurant with Boris.

"It is absurd, isn't it?" said Emilia.

"Oh, now you're offended. Don't be, please. It's just that"— Vanessa started laughing again—"I've been aiding in the corruption of a feminist professor."

"I'm afraid you've lost me."

"I'm an editor at LoveLorn."

This time the two women laughed together.

"As irony goes, this isn't bad," said Emilia. And with that, the mood of the afternoon shifted abruptly. Emilia, flustered, reached back to pat her hair, which had come undone.

"Want me to fix that?" Vanessa pulled out one of Emilia's sharp combs, releasing a tumble of thick hair, brown and streaked with new silver. Emilia closed her eyes. She felt Vanessa's cool fingers raking gently through her hair, repinning it, fluffing the tendrils around her brow and temples. "There," said Vanessa. "That's better."

"Thank you." Emilia looked at Vanessa without smiling. How long since someone had touched her hair? So long, too long, a long, long time ago.

They were silent for a moment.

"What I want to know is why ex-lovers can't just dry up and blow away," said Vanessa. "Why do they have to be walking around, breathing up air, living somewhere, seeing someone. Ex-lovers should all be shot. It should be a law." Then, mistaking the look on Emilia's face, she said, "I'm sorry. I don't know why I'm talking to you like this."

"Oh, please don't be sorry. I'm glad to be talking like this. I'm ... I also ... I wish the same thing about ex-lovers. I feel exactly the same way. There hasn't been anyone to talk to. There hasn't been anyone." Emilia's shoulders shook. Vanessa put her arms around Emilia.

"He's gone and married someone else," Emilia said, her voice muffled by Vanessa's bosom. "I'm sick of trying and trying and getting nowhere." She thought about her career; she thought about Serena, engaged to be married. It was all the same to her right then. There was nothing but emptiness.

And then there was awareness. Wet face, clothed bosom, softness against softness, cool hands on back of head, in hair, smooth warm hair over cold fingers, touching, touched, tentative contact.

SPELLS AND INCANTATIONS

~

Ophelia and Arthur were not going to the Halloween parade. They had made plans, along with two or three other people, to attend a private ceremony at a small cemetery in Queens. The ceremony was to be a spell-casting for the success of the Doomsday Coalition. Ophelia was dressed and ready to go, swathed in a black gown that revealed the white globes of her breasts, when Arthur came into her room with the dead chicken.

"Let me see it," said Ophelia. "Is it bloody enough?"

"I'll say it is," said Arthur. "It's dripping."

Ophelia looked into the brown paper bag, and promptly threw up.

VAMPIRE KISSES

~

Manya was watching a horror film on a tiny black-and-white television in her room. Although she was lying in bed with the covers over her, she was fully dressed, as she half expected some drunken hallmate to burst in on her at any time. "Just one brief moment of pain," said Count Dracula on the screen, "and then, eternal life!" As she watched the vampire lean over his victim's alabaster neck, closer and closer, Manya felt a shiver of something—fear?—run up her spine. The vampire's fangs hovered scant inches from the waiting feast ...

Her door slammed open and Manya screamed.

"I haf come to dreenk your bluuud," said Boris, waving his cape around.

"Boris! I could kill you!" Manya threw a pillow at him. "How did you get in here, anyway?"

"The cheel-dron of the night left the door open. I flew in on leettle bat wings."

"You could have been an ax murderer." Manya was ill at ease. She had not had a man in her room since the memorable night with Arthur.

"I am vurse than ax murderer," said Boris. "I haf come to make you like myself, one of the undead." He approached her, cape veiling his face below the eyes.

Manya laughed nervously and scrambled to a standing position. The bed, not built for such abuse, squealed in protest.

Boris stopped and assumed an expression of bewilderment. "You vill not be bride of handsome Slavic vampire?"

"No, I will most definitely not. Why are you really here?" Manya sat back down on the bed.

"Actually," said Boris, "I thought I'd check on the shop. Kids sometimes vandalize stores on Halloween, you know. So since I was going to be in Manhattan anyway, I decided to mix pleasure with business and scare you before dropping by Zaftigue. Want to come along?" What Boris was really doing in Manya's room, of course, was attempting to seduce her with humor.

"Dream on, Dracula," said Manya. She half suspected his real motive, but at eighteen, when your peers are out carousing, it is difficult to resist an invitation to join in some festivity. She was not fooled by Boris's offhand manner or his jocular attitude. She was not about to be seduced. But she was putting on her moccasin boots.

DINNER AS REVELATION
~

Guess who came to which dinner that night.

Pasta, served al dente, with a creamy tomato sauce and steamed vegetables; a light blush wine; a crisp Caesar salad with anchovies gleaming in oil; all of it touched with tentative forks and prodded by daring comments, interrupted by spurts of conversation and then by silence.

Chinese sesame noodles, fried dumplings, Szechuan beef, Extra-Delirious Chicken with Garlic; Tsingtao beer; appetizers eaten, main dishes all but ignored in favor of the fortune cookies, read with an attempt at humor, with an undercurrent of belief; laughter; talk that swirled around a central unspoken core like a tornado; hand holding; fear of bad breath.

Pepperoni pizza, vodka martinis, chocolate Yodels; a strong beginning marked with sardonic comments and casual verbal jousting between bites; an unexpected reaction, to the jousting or the pepperoni; a detour to the bathroom; a shocked reception upon return.

MENU NUMBER ONE

~

Emilia, elegant in black, her lips crimson and her hair arranged more loosely but still speared by sharp combs, lifted her glass and proposed a toast. She was eating tonight, real food, just as she would have if she'd gone out with a man. What did a day or so more off the program matter? She gave a mental shrug of her shoulders. Eat, drink, and be merry, for tomorrow we diet. She calculated Vanessa's height and weight with a practiced assessment of wrists and calves, and thought she might suggest that Vanessa join her on Slim Pickin's Mature Woman Maintenance. It certainly solved the problem of who would be cooking.

"Here's to creating our own romance," she said.

Vanessa, casting a nervous glance at the couple dining at the next table, obediently raised her glass. She was ruddy, her cheeks clashing with her hair, and appealingly wenchy in a low-cut orange silk blouse. The murmur of conversation and the clanking of cutlery assuaged her feelings of guilt and trepidation. She was used to being courted in restaurants.

"This is all so new to me," Vanessa said. "I never considered being involved with a woman before. Of course, now that I think about it, it makes perfect sense. Who understands a woman's needs better than another woman?"

Emilia nodded. She was a bit worried by the way Vanessa was nattering on. Now that she had made her decision to be intimate friends with another woman, with this woman, she was struck by little uncertainties. The spot of green on Vanessa's tooth, for example. And how intelligent was she, really?

Vanessa swallowed. Emilia seemed so remote and self-possessed—almost as much so as a man would have been. "A woman would intuitively know," she continued bravely, as was her fashion, "would intuitively know the symbolic importance of gestures, of little gifts, of talking things out. I just hate how men turn every conversation into an argument! Everything becomes a power struggle."

Emilia wondered if she could find the physical side of a female relationship satisfying. Can a person change her fantasies? Better not to say anything yet.

"But the thing I'm not sure about," said Vanessa, cracking her knuckles without thinking about it, "is how to shift gears. I mean ... I keep saying I mean, don't I? I mean ... oh, there I go again!"

The waiter, a young man whose handsomeness was marred by a strawberry birthmark on his cheek, hovered nearby, gauging their readiness for the next course, awaiting a lull in conversation.

"I mean, I've never known how it is that sex between two women could feel ... well, complete."

"Without penetration? I've wondered that myself."

The waiter cleared his throat. "Would you like coffee or dessert now?"

Having been a waitress herself, Emilia accepted this interruption with grace. "Any suggestions?"

The waiter paused. "Well, yes. I think you need to reframe the question. The real question, as I see it, is whether or not romance and sex need accompany each other at all. Personally, I've been faced with a similar dilemma myself, times being what they are. And if there needs to be sex, the question of what form it takes really boils down to the requirements of your imagination. The female body does not require penetration any more than the male does. You must renegotiate with your mind what you think your body demands. Now, we have eclairs, cannoli, and some rather excellent ladyfingers, or would you like another look at the menu?"

MENU NUMBER TWO
~

"Look," said Manya, "this one says, 'He who knows not that he knows knows what he knows not that he knows.' What do you think that means?" She was sitting on the floor of Zaftigue, toying with the remnants of their picnic dinner. Somewhere between the dumplings and the fortune cookies they had stumbled upon a romantic mood, and Manya was doing her best to dispel it.

"Damned if I know," said Boris. "Try this. 'A man who cannot forswear will ever be forsworn.'"

"Boris, you're holding my hand."

"I am aware of that fact." Boris looked out the window. The night sky had a reddish cast, an angry blush of color. "I think it's going to rain."

"Boris, why are you holding my hand?" Manya was enjoying herself too much to yank her fingers rudely from his grasp. She was also slightly drunk, and her reflexes—both mental and physical—were slow.

"We Russians are a very touchy people. If you and I can sit close to each other like this, if we can talk openly like this, then why can't we touch like this?"

"Boris, please don't be difficult." He was absently and expertly caressing her fingers, and Manya could feel the faint call of her flesh again, a wistful whisper of longing. It frightened her.

"Manya, what exactly is so difficult? We're friends. I know you. You get sad in the late afternoon. Your skin breaks out the day before your period. You were hurt by someone named Sally Shickelgruber. I know you well enough to know you trust me, or you wouldn't be here now."

"I do trust you. I trust you not to push me too far. Boris, don't pretend you don't understand what makes this difficult. It changes everything. You expect more from the person. You depend on them more."

"I could take a chance on that."

"Boris, you forget that I know you. You don't want someone depending on you. You want someone to be strong and unavailable. The only reason you're holding my hand right now is that I'm being strong and saying no."

"Then say yes and see if I let go."

Despite herself, Manya laughed.

"I can't promise you that everything will turn out perfectly, Manya. But that's not the point. It's like a journey." Boris raised her hand to his cheek and held it there, rubbing his stubbled jaw against her knuckles like a cat. "You should want to take this journey because of what you will find there, because it is a good place, even if it is not a perfect place."

The rain, at last, began to fall, in slow fat drops onto the sidewalk.

"Boris? You were right about the rain."

Boris distractedly turned her open palm so it cupped his face. "I was just trying to remember something my mother used to say about loving someone for the wrong reasons or the right reasons. Never mind. It will come to me. The part I do remember is this: the wrong reasons for a journey are to escape from something. Are you in love with someone else, Manya?"

"No," she said. "I'm not."

Thunder issued forth from the heavens, and it poured.

"Boris," said Manya, "I ..."

His lips claimed hers, and her arms crept around his neck, trembling. Boris's lips seemed too full, too soft; she recalled Arthur's kiss and was unmoved. *No*, she told her flesh, *don't do this now. Respond.* With a great lift of her spirit, she tried to summon up desire. She conjured desire with all her heart, and slowly at first, then with greater alacrity, her flesh obeyed.

What Boris had been trying to remember was something his mother had written in her diary the day her divorce was finalized. It went like this: "Loving someone for the right reasons is better than being loved for the wrong reasons. Being loved for the right reasons is better than loving someone for the wrong reasons. But by the time both of you love each other for the right reasons, one of you will probably be dead."

MENU NUMBER THREE

~

"What is it?" Arthur looked at Ophelia, thinking that she had never seemed less attractive. She was too thin, but her face was puffy and there were deep shadows of fatigue under her eyes. She had removed her black witch's gown, and underneath her white T-shirt her nipples were unusually prominent. They reminded him of udders.

"I threw up again." Ophelia's wry, husky voice was the only unchanged thing about her.

"I can understand how the sight of sacrificial chicken might make one ill, but the pizza wasn't that bad, was it?" Arthur looked around until his gaze settled on Ophelia's sketchbook propped against the wall.

"You tell me. Or rather, don't. I think you'd better leave."

"I don't have to go yet." Arthur stood up, lean and supple, to investigate the drawing.

"I think you should. Go, Arthur. Leave."

Arthur turned around just in time to see a fleeting expression of pain and something else, less easily defined, darken Ophelia's face like a cloud passing overhead. "Ophelia?" He did not know how to frame the question forming in his mind.

"Leave, Arthur, just leave." She was lying on her back on the mattressed floor, chanting almost, willing him away from her.

Arthur turned back to the sketch. "This is interesting," he said. "Very unlike your usual dark vision of things, wouldn't you say? What do you call it? *Woman Giving Birth to Flower*?"

"I call it a psychedelic experiment gone awry. Do you mind, Arthur? As Greta Garbo said before she was misquoted, 'I want to be left alone.'"

Arthur continued to study the sketch. "When did you do this?"

A sharp hiss of breath was her only answer.

"When, Ophelia?" He dragged the heavy artist's pad over.

"A week or so ago." Ophelia, not looking at Arthur or her self-portrait, placed her hands on her breasts.

Arthur put the pad down. "Do they hurt?"

"Yes." She allowed his gentle touch:

"Have you taken the test yet?"

"I'm writing a paper instead."

"Very funny. You should take the test. I'll go with you."

"Whatever for?" Ophelia looked at Arthur. "If I am, I'll have to schedule an abortion. You going to come along for that, too?"

"Are you sure that's what you'd want to do?"

"My dear sweet brainless, besides a possible new array of hormones, do you know what's zinging around in my bloodstream? Cocaine, nicotine, marijuana, acid, Ecstasy—you name it, it's in there. Then there's the little factor of me, likely to be voted least capable of producing or rearing a normal child. That's assuming that I'd want to consider nine months and eighteen years of mother-hell. Why? You want to marry me and raise a kid?"

"Ophelia."

"Arthur. What a poignant moment we're having." Then, seeing the look of utter helplessness on Arthur's usually impassive features, she relented. "Hey. You're really upset, aren't you?"

"What do you think?" Arthur bit out, more angrily than he'd intended. And then he rested his head against her shoulder, and cried.

Ophelia stroked his hair for a moment, deep in thought. "Arthur," she said after a pause. "Arthur. Please go now."

Sitting up, eyes red and sore, Arthur clenched and unclenched his hands on her shoulders, swallowing hard.

"Go," she commanded, with tenderness.

"I'm going," he said. "I'm gone." But still he sat there, unable or unwilling to move.

WAITER, I'D LIKE TO CHANGE MY ORDER

~~

Manya felt that a thin layer of oil had been transferred from the Chinese food to her skin. She didn't care. Outside Zaftigue, the rain still pattered down.

"It's funny, isn't it, after all this time? You and me. Who'd have thunk it?" She smiled and touched the slight valley in the center of Boris's narrow chest with her fingertips. The hair there was surprisingly sparse, straight and fine.

Boris looked grave. "I've cared for you for a while. You know that," he offered cautiously, sitting up. They were naked on the blanket that had held their picnic dinner not an hour before. Boris lifted a beer, drank, then looked in confusion at the other bottle. Which was his?

"Say more." Manya thought that the scene was going all wrong. Where had the teasing and camaraderie gone? It did not matter to her that they had not actually made love. They were flesh to flesh. She had surrendered to him. As far as she was concerned, they were lovers.

"What do you want me to say?" Boris drank again, no longer caring from which bottle. He had the darting, wary look of a cornered animal.

"I don't know," Manya said, although she knew precisely what she wanted to hear. Prospective lovers will tell each other exactly what they desire, but lovers who have shared unseen parts of themselves tend to rely on subtler forms of discourse.

"I think enough's been said for one night, don't you? We don't want to talk everything to death." Boris glanced at the clock. "Maybe I should be taking you home now."

"Boris, wait. Why are you pushing me away? Please look at me. What happened, is that what's bothering you?"

"Don't you mean what didn't happen?"

"But it shouldn't bother you. In a weird way, it made me happy. It proved to me that I am special to you. You couldn't take making love to me lightly, and making love—really making love—well, that's kind of frightening, isn't it? Isn't it?"

"Manya, you can't tell me all about this guy Arthur and expect me to have no reaction." Boris reached for his pants.

"But I thought you wanted me to be open. Besides, I know all about your women." It had seemed less courageous than necessary to tell Boris about Arthur; in order to begin the one, the true love affair, all veils had to be lifted, all lies and concealments dispersed like so much smoke.

"Come on, Manya, get dressed. I'll take you home."

Manya, on the verge of tears, hastily began to gather up her coat and bag. "I can get home very well on my own, thank you."

"Stop. No." Boris's hand on hers forestalled her. "This isn't a movie, Manya. I can't just come up with the right lines."

"You want me to leave. I'm leaving."

"Why are you making everything so difficult?" Boris closed his eyes. Women, he thought. He wanted to escape into his apartment, into Pushkin, into a bottle of vodka. Too much, too soon! How lovely the despair of wanting her had been, and now how awkward and overwhelming the reality of having her!

"You told me I was being difficult before, too," Manya reminded him. "But that was when I was being difficult because I didn't want to start anything tonight. Now I'm being difficult because I don't want you to throw me out." Manya disliked making her point this way; in her experience, which was of novels, people spoke plainly in fiction of the drugstore sort. In better literature, meaning was contained, not expressed. Only the certainty that silence now would contain an irrevocable ending kept her talking.

"I'm not throwing you out, Manya. I just need a little time to think. A day or two," Boris pleaded.

"You don't know what the hell you want, Boris," Manya said, surprising them both with her vehemence.

"Look, what am I supposed to do right now? You have the script, right? So what is supposed to happen?"

"Something! Something is supposed to happen afterwards!"

Manya and Boris glared at each other, and the harsh sound of her breathing recalled Boris to the first few moments when she had lain against him, her mouth to his ear, before she spoke and everything went wrong.

"Then give it time," Boris suggested with almost incongruous mildness.

"Oh, I'll give it time all right," said Manya. "I'll give it a long forever."

"Manya, don't be melodramatic."

"I thought you liked drama, Boris. But then, you change your mind so quickly it's hard to keep track. Not that it's my problem anymore."

"After we both have a chance to calm down, we can get together and …"

"Oh, have I mentioned that I quit? Well, I do. I quit you and I quit your crappy, stinking job. Dear me, is that the time? I think I'll go home now."

"Manya," said Boris, as if he were about to say more.

She stood up.

"Will you give it time? I didn't mean to hurt you. It's my fault. All of this is my fault. But just let me sleep on it, let me get my mind straight. I don't want things to end between us. Not like this."

"Too bad for you." Manya opened the door, hunting for other, better words of parting, words she knew would come to her only after she had left. What did the French call it? *L'esprit de l'escalier.* She gave Boris one last hurt and puzzled look, as if he might supply her with an answer; then she closed the door behind her.

Despite the Chinese food, she was voraciously hungry—for the feast of solitude, for a banquet of one. She quieted all the voices within her that clamored still for Boris's embrace, for his love and reassurance, with the promise of what she could, what she would give herself.

Manya might have been comforted to know that other hearts were broken that night. Elsewhere in the city, Herman Finder ate a frozen dinner and cried a little, because he was in love with Emilia and had missed his one opportunity to tell her so, and Cecile and Saul fought over cheap curry in the East Village, after which Saul decided to postpone his trip to France.

WHY YOU CAN'T
GO HOME AGAIN
~~

Manya woke up the next morning to find the raven of depression eyeing her balefully from the edge of her bed. No, there were two birds this time, one large and vigorously ill-tempered, the other weak, scrawny, and diseased. With these two familiars perched on her shoulders, Manya found that even the simplest tasks required a substantial investment of effort. Still, she managed to finish her midterm papers and exams over the next two days, pecked and prodded by ill temper, burdened by weakness.

At the end of this ordeal, Manya decided to go to Maplewood for the weekend. She wanted to be back where every object was homely and safe, wanted to be where her mother could coddle her with cooked suppers and irrelevant advice such as "Don't take things so much to heart" and "This is just part of growing up."

But Sophie had begun menopause during her daughter's absence. She had lost fifteen pounds and was much slimmer than Manya. She wore tight jeans and sweaters. She had dyed her hair black and then streaked it blonde. She told Manya that she was taking a night course in Jewish philosophy and attending morning mass at a Catholic church from time to time. She'd signed up for a singles weekend in the Catskills and had met a man there named Joel. Joel was twenty-nine.

Manya did not know what to do with this adolescent mother. She was an entirely changed creature, utterly possessed by her hormones. The old Sophie had been endlessly soft and maternal, ineffectual and kind. The new Sophie was moody, given to bursts of enthusiastic speech, fits of crying, phlegmatic silences, and complaints about the temperature. "Is it hot in here?" she asked Manya again and again. "It's November," Manya replied. "It's not hot." "Ah," Sophie would say every time, as if discovering the equator, "it's the flashes." She spoke constantly of bodily functions and death and sex; Manya learned more than she wished to know about her mother's state of vaginal lubrication, her intimations of mortality, and her plans to be buried under a flowering tree.

When Manya tried arguing in the old manner, accusing her mother of being contradictory, of not sending her to a better grade school or being a better role model or instilling her with more confidence, Sophie responded strangely. "I'm not the guiding force in your life anymore," she said. "It would be too easy for you to blame me. You have to have the courage to accept responsibility for yourself, Manya."

Feeling orphaned, Manya returned to New York on Sunday evening. She'd left home, and now home had retaliated by leaving her. How dare it all look so much the same and feel so different! And what was to become of her mother? Would she become a Catholic? Would she marry Joel? Manya did not waste much time worrying about these developments, however; Sophie belonged to a distant galaxy that had once been, but was no more, near the center of her daughter's universe.

Manya wandered back to her dormitory through a labyrinth of uncomfortable thoughts. Down one path was the disturbing question of whether or not she had ruined her chances with Boris by wanting too much certainty too soon. Should she just have allowed him time to think? She could not bring herself to believe that; it required too much trust. Manya tried another route, and the memory of Arthur, so recently loved and now loved no longer, brought her up short. What kind of person was she to drift from love to love as if shopping for the appropriate object? Manya turned a mental corner into a blind alley where, like a rat bent upon its own business, possessor of its own domain, a final terrifying thought presented itself. What if, rather than suffering from a confusing surfeit of love, she suffered from loving no one at all? Perhaps the only thing she wanted was to be loved; perhaps she wanted this so badly that her affections would jump into any passing stranger's arms. A rat. She was like a rat, voracious and omnivorous, able to squeeze through any emotional opening into which she could fit her head.

Manya stopped walking and had a revelation. It was a smooth revelation, sliding neatly into place, cold and silvery rather than radiant and golden. No, not silver, that was too soft and pliant a metal. It was steel, entering her soul and strengthening her resolve. Instead of cherubic angels, victorious Valkyries trumpeted their approval. What she needed now, Manya decided, was advice from someone cold and steely and warlike. What she needed, and pride be damned, was a strong dose of Ophelia.

THE INTRUSION OF A MINOR CHARACTER

~

Ophelia was in her room, but she was not alone. Her companion's face was familiar, although Manya could not immediately recall his name.

"Oh, it's only you," said Ophelia, not getting up from the mattressed floor. "Come in if you want."

Ophelia, Manya observed, was not looking her best. Her skin was pasty and gray, there were dark circles under her eyes, and most important, there was no aura of vitality emanating from her person. What force could have drained her, energy vampire that she was?

"I'm sorry to bother you," said Manya. "I could come back later if ..."

"I'm through here, so don't leave on my account," said the room's other occupant. Suddenly Manya remembered who he was: Misha Abramovich, campus activist, with his dark hair falling over his troubled, acne-scarred brow and fierce eyes glinting behind black-framed glasses.

Misha, who was working out plans for the Doomsday Coalition rally, also recognized Manya. He remembered her face, he realized, because of her peculiar resemblance to a lapdog. He had thought it unfortunate to have such a face; to Misha's taste, softness and vagueness were as repellent as leprosy. He was attracted by strength of feature. His women all had jutting foreheads, protruding noses, and massive shoulders. Mistakenly, people believed he did not choose his lovers on the basis of their looks.

Misha was the kind of person who is famous in college and far more famous after. The more famous he becomes, the better people knew him back when he was in their political science class. Manya looked at Misha and shivered, not with fear or attraction or distaste, but with the sudden awareness that here was a minor character in her life who would remain engraved in her memory. He had seen her and summed her up, and she would spend the next thirty years wondering what he had concluded about her. Then she remembered her revelation and lifted her chin one belligerent inch. *Do not presume to judge me*, she thought. *I am not what I appear!*

But Misha was looking at Ophelia. "Well, that's enough work for today. You know what you have to do for the rally, Ophelia?"

"Aye," said Ophelia.

"Excellent." Misha left swiftly and silently, as if accustomed to evading secret police.

There was a pregnant pause as the two women faced each other alone. Manya, of course, did not know how pregnant the pause really was.

"So," said Ophelia, examining the black polish on her toenails, "what brings you here?"

"I want to learn about men," said Manya, still standing.

"Interesting subject." Ophelia glanced up at Manya. She extracted a pack of cigarettes from between two mattresses, shook one out, and lit it. "You have my royal permission to sit, by the way. What's brought this sudden interest on?"

"I have come to the conclusion that falling in love is painful to oneself, while being loved is painful to the other person," said Manya. "I want to know how to make men fall in love with me without my falling in love with them."

DENATURE OF LOVE

~

The *Oxford English Dictionary* tells us that to denature is to alter a thing so as to change its nature. It can also mean to render alcohol, coffee, or tea unfit to drink, but that's neither here nor there. It is the first definition which concerns us. Who among us has not tried, at one time or another, to alter the nature of our emotions? The bookstores are filled with denaturing devices. *Stalking the Healthy Relationship. How to Stop the Codependency Duet. Turning the Wheel of Misfortune: How to Take Charge of Your Fate!*

Boris was trying to denature himself without the aid of a book. It was a messy job. He sat hunched over his desk, rubbing the still unfamiliar bareness of his chin, with only the headless torsos of mock-Greek women and one sullen mannequin for company. A bottle of vodka was his only anesthetic.

"I miss Manya," he said, refilling his glass, "and I miss my beard. Why did I shave it off? You'd think that a man who read about Samson and Delilah in the original Hebrew would have better sense."

The mannequin's grimly amused smile seemed to mock him.

"What are you so smug about, you dummy, you?" Boris drank his vodka down, saluting the mannequin with the empty glass. "Listen, dummy—no, let's give you a name. Lauren. Lauren Bacall. You look like her, you know, in that film—what was it?—*To Have and Have Not*. Listen, Lauren—no." Boris shook his head, trying to clear it. "This won't work. I can't bare my heart to a Lauren. It's too goyish a name. What was your real name, anyway? Beatrice? Bruriah? Betty? Okay,

Betty, why is it that when I thought Manya was in love with someone else, she seemed like the best thing that could ever happen to me? She seemed so gentle and sweet, and so damned smart, Betty. Wise beyond her years." Boris sighed deeply. "And probably wise beyond mine."

Betty's voice was clear and cool and mocking in his mind. "How poetic, Boris."

"Nu? Is this an answer?" Boris poured Betty a drink and handed it to her.

"Drink that for me, will you?" Betty's voice was husky, laced with secret feminine knowledge, innuendo, and suppressed laughter. "Thanks. I needed that. Listen, Boris. The first thing a man thinks when he sees a pretty girl is, How would she be in bed, and can I get her there? The second thing he thinks is, Is she the girl for me? Am I gonna marry her? The third thing he thinks is, What are the kids gonna be like? You got past question number one for the first time, and it scared you silly."

"That's a bit dated, isn't it, Betty? It's not 1944."

"Hey, the fundamental things still apply. Don't tell me Mr. Snake lost his strike just because some other jerk got there first."

"Watch your mouth, kid. You've been spending too much time with Bogie." Boris paused, his drink halfway to his mouth. "You may have a point. There was this moment when I looked at Manya and thought, There's someone whose face I could imagine mixed with mine, feature blended with feature in the face of a child, our child." Boris, embarrassed, searched his desk for cigarettes. "You don't by chance happen to have ..."

"As you said, it's not 1944. I quit the habit twenty years ago, when some kid ran into the shop where I worked and stole one of my hands."

"So why did I finally get past question number one with Manya?"

"Because she has quality. Because you're nearly thirty and that's one of the first ages of mortality. Because she's innocent in ways in which you're wise, and wise in ways in which you're innocent."

"How is she wise, my plastic philosopher?"

"She's wise in the ways of pain, friend."

"How is she innocent, then? In the ways of pleasure?"

The painted eyes flickered in a sudden shaft of moonlight, as if in agreement, or amusement, or both.

"But then why is it, Betty dear, that when Manya seems ready to fall into my arms, as plump and ripe a prize as any man could want, she suddenly seems eager and uncertain and just a little bit ridiculous, like a nervous puppy ready to do anything to accommodate its master?" Boris stood up, with some difficulty. "I'm goin' to try some pacing, Bets."

"Don't fall on your face."

Boris paced, carefully, across the floor. "As I see it, the problem is—hold on, the chair's in my way." Boris moved the chair. "The problem is, you fall in love and it feels fated, but it isn't fate at all, it's—it's—"

"Horribly random?"

"Yes. It's horribly random, and when you realize that it's chance and not fate, you can't really feel in love anymore. It's like falling in love with a puppy. All puppies are cute, the strays and the purebreds, and all puppies are pretty much the same, when you get right down to it. How do you choose one over the other? Why choose any at all?"

"Hmm." Betty hesitated, but only for a moment. "Boris, all puppies are not the same. They only seem the same for the first five minutes. After that, some pee on your leg, some lick your face, some bite your shoe, and some skulk off into a corner. Then you choose one. The puppy you choose eventually becomes your dog. And a dog which is your dog is dearer than all the puppies in the world which are not yours."

"But a person is not a dog, Betty. You don't go through life wondering if you chose the right dog, do you? What if I wake up one morning when Manya is pregnant with my child and wonder if I chose the wrong woman?"

"Instead of the right one? That would be a shame. Well, there's no problem, then. If there's a right woman out there for you, you would feel no doubts. You would see her and know instantly. We've solved the problem; if you have doubts about Manya, she's not the right woman."

"That's a dummy's reasoning for you. I have never come to anything in my life without doubts. I have doubts about what to wear in the morning. I had doubts about opening this shop. I have doubts about having this conversation with you. I mean, you really are exactly like thousands of other mannequins, even if puppies and women are different."

Oh, was that the wrong thing to say! Insulted, Betty fell silent, and became a thing of plastic and paint and fake hair again, rather than a tough broad with a ready supply of advice and an insinuating style.

"Talk to me, Betty," Boris pleaded. "I'll dress you in the finest silks! I'll buy you a new wig—replace your missing hand!" But Betty had said all she was willing or able to say, for her limits were those of Boris's imagination.

THE WAY OF A MAID
WITH A MAN

~~

Back in Ophelia's room, Manya was trying to lose the emotional layer of puppy fat which made her soft when she would be hard, playful when she would be tough. To this end, she had told Ophelia everything, from Arthur's seduction to Boris's rejection. Having confessed all, Manya felt a familiar rush of shame and relief. Divulging secrets, she thought, was a lot like vomiting.

"So then he wanted to get rid of you, right?" Ophelia dragged on her cigarette. "The oldest story in the book. 'Then up he rose, and donn'd his clothes, and dupp'd the chamber door; let in the maid, that out a maid never departed more. By Gis and by Saint Charity, alack, and fie for shame! Young men will do 't, if they come to 't; by Cock they are to blame. Quoth she, before you tumbled me, you promis'd me to wed: So would I ha' done, by yonder sun, an thou hadst not come to my bed.' Like that? It's from one of Ophelia's mad scenes."

"She sounds pretty lucid to me."

"Your problem is that you gave too much, that's all." Ophelia, finding herself in the altogether unfamiliar role of counselor, realized that there was something gratifying about helping someone in need. It made her feel in control again, and that feeling had been sadly lacking ever since her body's unexpected betrayal.

"Gave too much? You mean sleeping with him—them?" Manya had decided to be as brave in the pursuit of questions outside the classroom as she was inside. She rested her chin on her fist and resisted the urge to take notes.

"Gave too much of yourself. You can give your body if you hold your affection in reserve. You can give your affection if you withhold your body. But if you give both affection and body, men tend to become overwrought with ambivalence."

"But why, Ophelia? What is love if it isn't giving freely of yourself? What do men want, if they don't want love?"

Ophelia thought about this. Her way with men was instinctive; she had never put it into words before. "It's like this, Manya," she said. "Men feel about losing their space the way women feel about losing their virginity."

"Space? What kind of space?"

"Inner space. The space to do whatever they want whenever they want. The space to be themselves without having to expend any emotional energy whatsoever. This is why men tend to have the upper hand in relationships. Women want affection, and men want space. But women want affection from men, and men want space away from women. That's why it's a bad idea to give too much of yourself to a man. It crowds them. They go all panicky."

"How did you get to know so much about men?" asked Manya.

Ophelia's pale face glowed with some of its former vampiric intensity. "Because I'm one of the rare exceptions to the rule. I'm a woman who wants space. This is the real secret to mastering men, Manya. When a man meets a woman who wants space more than he does, he starts wanting affection. And then who has the upper hand?"

SHE LOVES ME,
I LOVE HER NOT
~

When you are in love with someone who does not love you, you wish that the roles could be reversed. But it's not that easy, being loved by someone whose affections you cannot return. It's like being trapped in a lecture, wishing to leave unobtrusively but knowing you can't. You don't want to hurt anyone's feelings; you pray for an intermission during which you can sneak out the back.

Vanessa had been lecturing for two weeks, and Emilia was still waiting for an intermission.

"Talking with you is so easy," said Vanessa. "I say something about myself and you really listen. With men, I always wound up listening to them telling me about themselves." Vanessa was sitting cross-legged on Emilia's floor, admiring Emilia's old Persian carpet and thinking how nice it must be to have a family that gave you nice things. Vanessa did not know that Emilia's mother had given her the carpet on the anniversary of her father's third year of silence; after seven years had passed since father communicated with daughter, Emilia received the antique rosewood bureau that stood in her bedroom. In fact, Vanessa knew very little about Emilia.

"Here," said Vanessa. "Careful, it's strong."

"Hmm," said Emilia, taking the joint. "Somehow, I can't imagine you just sitting there, listening." Emilia had mentioned that she'd never smoked grass in college, and Vanessa, to Emilia's surprise, had produced a bag of the stuff as casually as if it were a bottle of wine. Emilia discovered that she liked being stoned. It made ordinary, rather boring things seem new and fascinating. An egg was the ovoid container of mutable reality. A glass of milk became a thick substance redolent of fetal murmurings. The pattern on the Persian rug was transformed into an oscillating landscape. Vanessa's endless prattle became almost endurable.

"But that's just what I did, Emilia. I listened while men talked on and on about how they'd come to be the marvelous creatures they were. With you, I find myself exploring whole new regions of self. I surprise myself with the things I say. I'm discovering myself with you."

But a person couldn't stay stoned for the course of an entire relationship, Emilia thought. At least she couldn't. Being stoned had seen her through two weeks of Vanessa, had made making love seem like a long, gentle wave that never quite broke on shore, but it had also made getting up the next morning extremely difficult. And then there was the problem of teaching. Emilia had found herself teaching at least three classes while stoned. It was so hard not to go off on a tangent, and though banal things suddenly seemed exciting to her, they obviously did not strike her students in the same manner. If only the students were stoned, the way they used to be!

"Sometimes, Vanessa, and please don't take this the wrong way, I wish we could speak about something other than you." Emilia sat on her heels, dressed in faded jeans, a white T-shirt, and a jade silk kimono. Her beauty shimmered like the flame of a durable candle set in a strong draft. Vanessa was the draft.

"What do you mean, talk about something else?" Vanessa inhaled deeply, held her breath, and regarded Emilia with a hurt expression. Then she exhaled and said, "You talk about yourself, too, don't you? Aren't you learning things about yourself with me?"

"Yes," said Emilia carefully, "but aren't there times when you feel that we are really more suited as friends than as lovers?"

"I don't believe you're saying this! I don't feel that way at all, Emilia, and if you did you owed it to me to give me some sort of warning ..."

Knock, knock, ding, ding, knock, ding. Whoever was at the door was taking no chances.

Vanessa and Emilia looked at each other.

"Who can it be?" asked Emilia.

"It's your apartment," said Vanessa.

"I'm too elevated to deal with someone I don't know," said Emilia, with dignity.

"If they're at the door, they're probably someone you know," replied Vanessa. Ungrammatically, as Emilia could not help but note.

"I'm not prepared for this," Emilia admitted as she rose unsteadily to her bare feet. She opened the door with the chain still attached. "Who is it?"

"It's me," said Serena.

Emilia closed the door, unlatched the chain after two attempts, and let Serena in.

"I'm sorry, I'm sorry, bursting in on you like this. I'm sorry," said Serena, nervously stroking the fur coat she held in her arms as if it were alive and needed soothing. The fur, unsoothed, shed a few dark blond tufts onto the floor.

"Serena! What's happened?" Emilia listened anxiously to her own voice. Did she sound stoned? Her heart raced for a moment, and then she noticed that the Tiffany diamond was conspicuously missing from its roost on her friend's ring finger.

"Should I leave?" asked Vanessa tartly.

"Oh, I'm intruding!" Serena looked down at Vanessa on the rug, taking in the ashtray and the joint, and clapped her hands together in dismay.

"No, Vanessa, don't go. And of course you're not intruding, Serena. What's the matter?"

"I've broken up with Jack. No, that's a lie. Jack's broken up with me." Serena sank down onto her knees and pulled a few loose hairs from her coat.

"That's a man for you," said Vanessa, "trouble on wheels. Do you want some grass?"

"How did it happen, Serena?" Emilia was already sorry that she'd told Vanessa to remain. At any moment Vanessa might say something incriminating, and then Emilia would be forced to acknowledge that this embarrassing woman was her lover.

"Grass! I haven't smoked in years. Thanks," said Serena, taking the proffered joint from Vanessa and lighting it with a return of her habitual self-possession.

Emilia decided to forestall any revelations Vanessa might have in mind. "Serena, this is Vanessa, an editor at LoveLorn. Vanessa, this is Serena, an old friend of mine."

"Someone broke up with me recently, too," said Vanessa.

"Oh?" Serena sniffled. "What happened?"

"He fell in love with someone else. Someone younger else."

"I suppose it's biological," said Emilia, thinking of Saul and Cecile.

Serena shook her head. "Not with Jack. It wasn't someone. It was something. And it was so sudden! We were sitting in my mother's backyard in Westchester, planning out the wedding, when I mentioned wanting a band of strolling medieval minstrels with lyres and bagpipes. Jack threw a fit, yelling about conspicuous consumption and unnecessary expenses. I said this was my fantasy, my chance to play out my dreams, and he said, 'No, it's a wedding, our wedding.' He said I had to face facts, and the fact was that a new intern didn't make what an actuary did."

"What's an actuary?" asked Vanessa, chewing on her cuticle.

"I don't know exactly," said Serena. "It's something like an accountant, but harder to explain. Basically they deal with numbers, take lots of tests, and make tons of money, and Jack used to be one before he changed careers and got into medicine."

"I believe," said Emilia with stoned precision, "that an actuary is a statistician who looks over historical data and makes calculations of probability and risk. From these projections ..."

"Thank you for that timely report, Ms. Larsdatter. What happened then?" Vanessa asked Serena.

"Then we started fighting, and Jack said that he never knew I was so materialistic and that he was trying to get away from that sort of thing. Is it materialistic to want a nice wedding? Is it materialistic to want romance?"

"What on earth does a hugely expensive wedding have to do with romance?" asked Emilia. "Romance is spontaneous. Romance is the transformation of the quotidian into the sublime. A wedding, on the other hand, is a cultural and religious ritual instituted so that society has increased control over an individual, the disposal of an individual's wealth, and the procreation of offspring."

"What book did you get that from?" Vanessa, like Emilia, had thrown off the soporific effects of the pot, but the drug still worked in their bloodstreams, lowering inhibitions. "Not from one of those romance novels you love to read—they end in marriage."

"You've just supported my case, Vanessa. Romance ends in marriage. I can see why, in traditional societies, a woman might invest her wedding day with great meaning—it is the one day when she is celebrated, considered of value—but I fail to comprehend why you would put so much importance on some Scarlett O'Hara fantasy, Serena."

"Oh," said Serena, "why don't *you* call Jack up, Emilia? That's exactly what he said. I'm sure the two of you would be very happy together!"

Vanessa nodded her head, shaking her red hair vigorously. "I agree with Serena. You talk about romance as transformation. Why shouldn't a woman want to be transformed for one day? What's so wrong about making a wedding a bit of a production? No one comes down on movie directors for staging lavish crowd scenes with glitter and hoopla. Think of a bride as a movie director who gets to star in her own creation."

"Exactly! Now, why can't Jack understand that?" Serena heaved a sigh. "Sometimes I think men are a different species entirely. Maybe I should marry another woman."

"It's just as difficult with a woman," said Vanessa.

"Is it really? I would have thought that there would be a kind of unspoken understanding. I always feel like I have to translate things for men. With another woman, you have such a strong common bond. You could sit around together eating chocolate right before your period and be grouchy. You could stay up all night talking about emotions. Men always want a conversation to have a point. Hey—do you think that's phallic thinking?" Serena giggled, took the joint from the ashtray, and relit it. "The only thing is, I find the thought of sleeping with another woman kind of gross." Serena took a deep drag on the joint and held it in. "I mean, what would you do? You couldn't really do much, could you?" She exhaled a plume of smoke, which blew toward Vanessa.

Emilia, catching the look on Vanessa's face, tried to intervene. "Serena, it's a proven fact that everyone has at least the potential to be bisexual."

"Are you?" Serena laughed. "I'm sure as hell not."

"Everyone is," said Vanessa, "whether they admit to it or not."

"I'd rather be celibate for the rest of my life than sleep with a woman," said Serena. "It's not that I'm prejudiced. There's just no attraction. Could you be attracted to a woman, Emilia? Really attracted?"

Vanessa's raucous laugh provided the answer.

Ding, ding, knock, ding, knock, knock, knock! A night of anxious callers was obviously in the making.

"I'll get it," said Emilia, glad of the distraction. Glad, that is, until she opened the door.

"Hello, Em," said Saul, standing there in an olive-green army jacket, his graying red hair askew and his look of a maddened biblical king softened by a vague, unhappy expression. To Emilia, he seemed to appear as if through a gauze-covered lens. The effect was flattering.

Emilia leaned on the door. "Hello, Saul." She felt exhausted. He must have sensed that her energy reserves were dangerously low. His timing had always been perfect that way; he would have made a good predator.

Saul cleared his throat. "Here," he said. He'd brought a bouquet of purple flowers. They looked wilted, but their decay brought out the fullness of their scent.

"I have people here." Emilia held the flowers away from her face. The smell of them made her feel more stoned.

"So I see. I just wanted to tell you—Cecile and I are finished. My defeat, your victory."

"Ah." Emilia had no idea what to say. What was the appropriate response? Her mind was flowing thickly from thing to thing. Vanessa, watching with her vulgar hennaed hair and her heavy hands—would she never stop biting her cuticles? Serena, distracted from her grief by this drama. The joint, about to spill its ashes on her rug.

"I'd like to talk, Em. I need to talk with someone who knows me well."

"I'll probably wind up sympathizing with Cecile. That's how well I know you."

Saul's laughter was as intimate as a kiss. It brought a hot flush to Emilia's cheeks. "That's my Emilia, honest as a slap in the face. Can I call you?"

"You may."

"Will you see me?"

"I might."

Saul started to leave, then looked back over his shoulder. "Nice to see you, Serena," he called. "Nice almost meeting you, Red."

Emilia stood there for a moment after he'd gone, holding the flowers up to her face.

"Wasn't he nice," said Vanessa. Her voice was hard.

"My, my—Saul, after all this time. Speaking of time, it's getting late. I suppose I'd best be getting home. Want to share a cab, Vanessa?" The question was phrased just a little too archly.

Vanessa shook her head. "No, I'm staying here."

"Are you really?" Serena turned to Emilia. "What fun. A sleepover!"

"Not exactly," said Vanessa in a firm tone of voice.

"Because you are going home, Vanessa," said Emilia, in an even firmer tone of voice.

"I think we need to talk, Emilia."

Serena looked from Vanessa to Emilia and then back again. "Oh, dear, I really did intrude tonight, didn't I? You could have told me, you know."

"Told you what?" Emilia, holding Saul's bouquet, walked over to the kitchen.

"That you're a lesbian." Her voice trembled slightly with outrage. "It's not that I mind, but after all, we're friends. To think of how I've rambled on about fixing you up with some man!"

Emilia, wielding a sharp knife, whacked off the ends of the stems. "Oh, Serena, lighten up. For someone who's had more lovers than Messalina, you've gotten awfully conservative lately. Besides, I'm not a lesbian."

"Are you telling me that there's nothing going on here between you and Vanessa?"

"Yes," said Vanessa. "What are you trying to say?"

"Vanessa, perhaps we should talk, but tonight is not the night for it. I can't take any more right now."

"I suppose I'll go home and nurse my broken heart," said Serena, gathering up her fur, which was curled in a heap on the rug.

"I suppose I will, too," said Vanessa, getting her coat from the closet. "I can lend you a good romance novel if you'd like. The best romances are in books, anyhow."

Finally alone, Emilia ran tap water into a vase, humming softly under her breath. She arranged the slightly wilted purple flowers with a few deft touches and left them on the kitchen counter.

Halfway down the hall, she retraced her steps, picked up the vase, and brought it with her into the bedroom.

LITTLE JANIE SAUNDERS
AND DR. DEATH

~~

Ophelia dragged deeply on her cigarette and looked over the letter she intended to send to the *New York Times:* "The Doomsday Coalition will hold a rally at Columbia University on December 21 in order to draw attention to the apocalyptic situation in New York City, where the proliferation of drug-related crime and the issue of the homeless ..."

Ophelia flipped to another letter, this one earmarked for a sensationalist pseudo-news television show: "This rally signifies a return of the values of the 1960s. The pendulum is swinging back from safe sex and just say no to drugs. Prohibition has been in effect long enough! The youth of America demands that the establishment-oriented tidal wave that began with antiabortion campaigns and has swept free speech along in its wake ..."

Ophelia skimmed the rest and then turned to the next letter. For the various television news networks, there was an emphasis on the visual: torrents of protesters, young and old, babes in arms, professors in robes, students in death's-head costumes carrying giant placards and pounding on drums and tambourines.

For the *Village Voice,* there was mention of the student-spawned revolutions in China, Rumania, and Czechoslovakia.

For Greenpeace, there was a veiled suggestion that the Doomsday Coalition had stolen a small cache of plutonium which was to be used to hold the United States government hostage until it shut down all nuclear power plants presently in operation.

Satisfied, Ophelia stubbed out her cigarette. She folded the letters neatly, slipped them into preaddressed envelopes, and licked them shut, fighting a wave of nausea at the taste. Then she removed her grandmother's ivory silk wedding gown from her closet, ran her fingers over its yellowed lace trim, and very deliberately sliced her finger with a sculptor's tool. As the blood trickled down onto the aged silk, she moved her hand to make the pattern larger.

"Have you a daughter?" she whispered to herself as she worked. "Then let her not walk i' the sun, for if the sun breed maggots in a dead dog ... conception is a blessing ... but not as your daughter may conceive."

Everything Ophelia had ever wanted to know, she had found in *Hamlet*. All her creative madness, her blunt coquetry, her vision of humanity and her attitude toward death, were inspired by that play, so it was no wonder she found further education superfluous and the thought of long life absurd. She did not question the purpose and meaning of her existence, for she had chosen a purpose and meaning, and was content. But lately she was tired, physically tired. Often she sat sphinxlike in one place for an hour, half aware of the churning activity inside her womb. It seemed to her that she was not entirely in accord with herself. Foolish womb, Ophelia thought, to occupy itself thus while she planned her suicide!

No sooner had she thought this than Death arrived.

"Lovely outfit," he said, crossing his legs and hitching up his voluminous black robes. "I suppose you're planning on wearing it to our wedding?"

"As a matter of fact, I am," said Ophelia.

"A pregnant bride. How charmingly immoral." Death tapped his pipe against the wall. "Yet somehow I get the feeling that you're having second thoughts. Could it be that my rival has staked a claim on you?"

"What rival?" Ophelia, finished with her design, sucked on her finger.

"I think you know. Or is your brain getting a bit sluggish these days? Why don't you have an abortion, Jane?"

"Don't call me that. And why should I? It's a bit beside the point, don't you think?"

"Hmm." Death inserted the pipe into the cowled darkness that could not, by any stretch of the imagination, be called a face. "You realize that you won't be able to dye your hair again until the baby's born. What's your real color, anyway?"

"Light brown. But this baby's not going to be born."

"Oh, come off it, Jane. You can't lie to me. I can smell Life on you. Life's seeped into your pores and sapped your will. You aren't going to kill yourself. I usually keep this information confidential, Jane, but in your case I'll make an exception. You won't die until you're an octogenarian."

"Ophelia. My name is Ophelia."

Dr. Death laughed. "Foolish child, don't you see what I'm trying to tell you? You wanted to kill Ophelia. Well, Ophelia is dying. But Jane lives, and shall live—a good long time."

"What do you mean?"

"You've changed, Jane. Look at yourself. You look quite sweet and gentle and—do pardon the pun—just a teeny bit plain, Jane, in your new maternal incarnation. Look at the drawings you've been doing lately. Flowers, babies, vibrant colors. You help Manya out with no ulterior motive."

"I'm still working on the Doomsday Coalition."

"But you're avoiding Arthur, aren't you? Feeling a little frightened of the boy now that he's begun to sprout a few emotions?"

"Oh, shut up."

"If you insist on souring the milk of human kindness and going ahead with your plans, perhaps you should try out a bit of Lady Macbeth. 'I have given suck, and know how tender 'tis to love the babe that milks me: I would, while it was smiling in my face, have pluck'd my nipple from his boneless gums, and dash'd the brains out, had I so sworn as you have done to this.'"

"Whatever your heart desires, sirrah. 'Come to my woman's breasts, and take my milk for gall, you murdering ministers'! How's that? But as I recall, the lady wound up as an obsessive-compulsive with a hand-washing fetish."

"Very pert, very clever. And they say one shouldn't mock Death! It's always troubled me how no one credits me with having a sense of humor. I'm really a very funny fellow when I'm not functioning in my official capacity. Ah, well. I see you're getting exasperated. Shall I allow you to convince me? There's an idea. Here, take my hand." Death stretched out his darkness until it nearly touched Ophelia's warm flesh.

"Not now! Later, at the rally. I don't want to die now."

"But why? Quitting life is like quitting smoking, my dear. There's never any point in putting it off. Take my hand."

"Not yet! I need another month to prepare." Ophelia tucked her hands into her chest. Her heart was pounding with blood that flowed through embryonic pathways. "What good would it do me to die now? I need a sensational exit. I don't want to depart this life without leaving a ripple. It's not oblivion I'm after, it's immortality. Oh, don't even say it. First of all, I don't consider propagation a solution. As far as I'm concerned, the urge to reproduce has nothing to do with an individual's desire to live on in some way, it has to do with a species instinct to survive. And as for my art, I look around me and see that every Tom, Delia, and Harry here on campus thinks they're going to be a famous writer, artist, or scientist. Do you know what most of them are going to be? Advertising executives, lawyers, robots and drones. Two years after graduation all the would-be heroes will be at their desks worrying about next Tuesday's deadline. That's not for me. I'm not going to accept that fate. I'm not even going to take the chance, because the real death is a life of mediocrity."

"My poor child, every mortal must take that chance. Haven't you considered that even a sensational death will occupy no more than a minute on the evening news and then be forgotten? Not that it will matter to you any longer. One small benefit I grant my clients is this: when you cease to exist, you also cease to care. Silly chit. I've lost patience with you. Take my hand now or resign yourself to life."

"But there's no point to dying now!"

"All right. Fine. That's your decision." Death lifted his arm and consulted an hourglass strapped to his sleeve. "I believe our session has ended, Jane, and I do have other appointments today. I'll send you the bill in sixty years or so, when your soul has acquired a bit of interest."

With that, Death stepped from his armchair into a ring of stones and tapped his pipe against his palm to release a few sparks. Death tapped again, this time producing a blazing fire which consumed him until he was no more than a pillar of hot ash crumbling rapidly onto a mattress, leaving only a few small burn marks that looked as if they could have been made by cigarettes.

BEARDING THE BORIS
IN HIS DEN

~~~

Everyone wants to surrender to a belief, especially the young. They are daring that way. The reason older people tend to hesitate before surrendering to a belief is that it is dangerous. Jump out of an airplane and you may fall to your death; jump into a belief and you may fall into despair. The young are willing to take that risk. Their desires run hotly through their veins, and the desire to believe is one of the strongest desires known to humankind.

Boris had told Manya that it was worthwhile to take a chance on him, and she had believed him. He had ignited hope in her breast and then extinguished it. Now she needed a new belief, a new hope. Her selection was a popular choice: the belief that one should don a good suit of armor to protect the vital organs and emotions, and go around vanquishing people. Manya was through with wanting to be an object of desire. She was ready for battle, with Boris as both opponent and prize.

Manya gave herself a week to prepare. During that time, she compiled a mental scrapbook consisting of:

Ophelia's tuneless singing and off-the-cuff quoting
Professor Larsdatter's heel-swivel maneuver
Lauren Bacall's knowing look and husky one-liners
Sally Shickelgruber's amused arch of the left eyebrow
Michelle Pfeiffer's wide-eyed blend of poise and innocence
Arthur's rueful smile and sardonic shrug

In addition, she bought the following items:

1 tube bright red lipstick
book of popular quotations
sexy black brassiere and matching panties
Dunhill cigarettes
1 pair dangling rhinestone earrings
tape of 1960s French pop songs
black "fuck me" pumps
red sweater to fall off shoulder
Italian fashion magazine

Manya smoked Dunhills until their taste half appealed to her, and walked around her room in the black pumps every day for two hours to the accompaniment of 1960s French pop songs. She practiced arching her eyebrow, swiveling on her heel, and saying things like "Desire goes best with a cold drink and a hot bath" with a rueful smile and a sardonic shrug. She memorized quotations about men, women, love, and sex, studied flirtatious poses from the Italian fashion magazine, and discovered how to smile so that a dimple appeared in the middle of her right cheek. When she could walk, swivel, quote, arch, shrug, smile, and smoke without falling, stuttering, blinking, coughing, or feeling like a complete idiot, she knew that she was as ready as she would ever be.

To insure that Boris would be less ready than she, Manya gave him no warning, walking into Zaftigue as she had that first time, as any shopper would, with the unstated expectation of being served.

Manya sat at her usual perch atop the stool, swinging one

foot until its black high-heeled pump fell with a clatter to the floor.

"It's good to see you again," said Boris. "I think you've lost your shoe."

"I'm airing the toes on that foot," Manya corrected him. "Mind if I smoke?"

Boris lit her cigarette. There was a quizzical expression on his face, particularly around the eyebrows and mouth. "Would you also like a drink?"

"Desperately. So, how have you been getting on, Boris?" Manya arched an inquisitive eyebrow.

"I've missed you," Boris said, holding both bottle and glass aloft as he poured. "But the time alone has been good for me. I've been doing a lot of thinking." He handed Manya the glass and retreated to his desk, where he arranged himself in a posture halfway between sitting and standing.

"Cheers, Boris." Manya downed the vodka in one graceful gulp, without choking. She'd practiced that, too.

"*Nasdarovya.*" Boris sipped his vodka slowly. "Are you sure you're all right?"

Manya gave a small shiver, brought her shoulders together, leaned forward to reveal cleavage, threw back her head, and laughed low in her throat. "Did you think I'd be heartbroken? Really, darling, give a girl some credit."

"But I behaved abominably."

"Which is to say you acted like a man. As Françoise Sagan said, 'I like men to behave like men. I like them strong and childish.'"

"Manya, stop this act. I want to talk to you."

"Then talk to me." Manya licked her lips.

Boris took a moment to hoist himself up until he was completely seated on the desk. "I know I hurt you. I know I hurt you badly. I wish I could just take it all back, but I can't. And to tell the truth, even though I care for you, I know I can't promise that I won't wind up hurting you again." He leaned forward and cupped his head in his hands. "I suppose I have a hang-up about commitment, and maybe that's the reason I can't tell whether what I feel for you is enough or will last. I don't even know whether what I feel for you is love. But I do know that I care for you enough to be honest." Boris looked up again. His face had never been more pale, pointed, earnest, or handsome.

"I suppose you expect me to gasp now," she said, "or shed a few tears. But all you're saying is that you're ambivalent. You might as well say that you're breathing. It's no big surprise to me. I understand ambivalence."

"You don't understand. I don't want to take a chance on hurting you again. We can't be involved that way. I suppose it's even for the best that you quit your job here."

Manya, who had replaced her shoe, walked toward Boris, swiveled on her heel, and regarded him over one shoulder. "It's too late for that, Boris. We are involved."

"No, Manya," Boris said, "we're not."

"Do you think saying makes it so? We're involved whether you agree or not." Manya turned to face him. "And no offense, but I think you overestimate the potency of your charm. You're not going to hurt me. You're my friend. I'm very fond of you. I'm sure I'll like going to bed with you as soon as you get over your little problem."

"I didn't have a problem, Manya. I had an attack of scruples."

"Or is it that you didn't find me attractive?" Manya's voice had just the right tinge of arrogant amusement.

"You know I did. I still do."

Manya stepped closer, until her lips were scant inches from his. Her heart was pounding at his admission, but she kept her breathing even.

"Manya, don't. This is a bad idea."

"Is it?" Manya paused a moment, her face immobile. "Perhaps you're right." She walked back to the stool, heels clicking against the floor. "Let's forget the whole thing. I'll start back to work as usual this weekend."

"Please," Boris said, nearly groaning. "Why are you forcing my hand this way? I don't want to be brutal, but I suppose I'll have to be. You can't come back to work here."

"Why? What's the problem? You say no sex, that's fine with me. We had a flirtation, it went nowhere, end of story. I have no difficulty with that."

"Are you sure? We'll just be friends?"

"Just friends." Manya walked to the door. "But as you once said to me, if you do happen to discover that you're in love with me, we'll renegotiate our relationship. See you Saturday," she said gaily, and left.

The moment she stepped out of Zaftigue, Manya slumped. Her feet trembled in their black pumps, her throat ached from cigarettes, and her head spun miserably from the vodka. One of the reasons people envy actors is that their performances are recognized as such and can be applauded. For Manya, there was no audience save the superego, and the superego is a notoriously critical observer. Yet Manya's performance deserved applause, for her clown prince had refused to play his part properly, and still she had gone on with the scene. Having taxed herself to the limit of her powers, Manya found herself wondering if and when she would be rewarded for all her effort.

PROLEGOMENON TO BULIMIA

~

Binging is the result of an emotional equation that can be expressed in this manner: **self-esteem − demands of the world = need for immediate gratification.**

Self-esteem, which can be likened to a particularly temperamental houseplant, can wilt and turn brown in a matter of moments; it usually requires days of careful tending before it returns to its green and thriving state.

Demands of the world include: the slings and arrows of outrageous fortune; academic and/or job pressures; social interaction; rejection; and attempting to act blithely sophisticated with lovers who tell you with quiet concern that they do not want you anymore.

Immediate gratification, in this context, refers to any food for which a nutritionist would substitute carrots. Now, if the **need for immediate gratification,** once gratified, resulted in a **higher level of self-esteem,** there would be no problem. Unfortunately, this is not the case. The **need for immediate gratification,** once gratified, results in a lump of undigested food in the stomach and the nagging prospect of imminent weight gain. Imminent weight gain results in an even **lower level of self-esteem,** and that, clearly, is to be avoided at all cost. Therefore it is incumbent upon the bulimic to **reverse the binging equation.** Any questions?

Manya had a question. *Why must I do penance for the simple business of living in the world?* Poised over the porcelain rim of the toilet bowl, Manya found herself reluctant to continue as she formed an altogether unpleasant association between the task she was performing and the surroundings in which she was performing it. The expression "eating shit" came forcibly to mind. It was the proximity of mouth to toilet, she thought. No matter how organized she was, no matter how quick and efficient, there was something taboo about deliberately kneeling where others squatted. She paused to consider the ramifications of this.

Creak, creak. Someone was coming into the bathroom. Quickly, Manya rose from her knees inside the stall and, sacrificing the cleanliness of her skirt to the necessity of the moment, sat on the open toilet.

Rough male voice number one: "It was so dark out there I could barely see you. Damn. But when you threw me that ball I thought for sure that Chuck was going to intercept. Could you see what ..."

Rushing water, splashing sound, short bark of laughter.

Rough male voice number two: "Yeah, yeah, and then he fell back, right? Ouch. I got a scrape on my leg like you wouldn't believe."

Number one: "I'm not gonna take a shower now. I'm gonna take a shower in the morning."

Number two: "I'm gonna take a shower now."

Number one: "Naw. Look, let's go, and then we'll ..."

The door slammed blessedly shut, and there was silence.

Manya remained seated on the toilet, perspiring heavily in the humid confines of the stall, too conscious of the distended burden of food in her belly to leave. Nervously, she listened for the sound of the door until she was overcome with the fatigue particular to those who stand sentry. She thought about going back to her room and sleeping until her belly was empty again—three hours, six hours, a day?

'No, it was unthinkable. She had to finish what she'd started.

But who will want to kiss these lips? She thought of Boris and did not feel that she would ever brave his face close to hers again.

INDIGESTION

~~

What repels us has the power to move us, and this explains a good many relationships. "What does he see in her?" "Doesn't she know that he's disgusting?" If only we could place love by special order, with sufficient advance warning to the chef! Then love would always be wholesome, healthful, and appealing. But it cannot be so. Love, romantic love, is a delicacy, and like most delicacies, it has the power to appall. Snails in burnt butter, the legs of a frog, fish eggs, small-boned birds, tentacles, monkey brains, bivalves killed on the plate— have you noticed that many gourmet items sound like ingredients in a witch's brew?

In order for love to be passionate, there must be turbulence—the soul's version of indigestion.

Emilia called Saul. Not by phone—she didn't have his number. But she called him forth from the depths of her imagination, where he had been hibernating, dormant but never dead. He rose up in her thoughts like a bear after the long winter of her celibacy, and she was so hungry for him that she not only found herself eating snacks between meals but also meals between snacks. When he finally rang, a week and a half after he dropped by her apartment, the flowers he'd brought had turned black and Emilia had trouble keeping her voice from trembling with excitement.

"We could meet at the Chinese place on my corner. I finish teaching at one."

"So I'm not welcome in the sanctum sanctorum, your apartment?"

"I didn't say that."

"Keep it all at a safe distance? Jesus, Emilia, I thought we were friends by now."

"Saul, why do you insist on misconstruing me? All I meant was, it might be nice to meet on neutral ground at first."

"Why not a bank in Switzerland? Is Switzerland neutral enough for you?"

They wound up meeting in Emilia's apartment. Emilia wore an unstructured gray knit suit she'd bought to accommodate her recent weight gain. On an impulse, she had gone to the hairdresser and had her hair cut to chin length. Every time her hand strayed to it, she was filled with a spasm of doubt. Too many changes, too fast, and how to tell if they were good ones or bad? Did her face appear fatter now, or did the bob conceal her puffy cheeks? Saul, confident in a dirty white jeans jacket that strained over his potbelly, took off his sneakers and waggled his toes.

"You're looking yourself," he said. He downed half the glass of beer Emilia had brought in from the kitchen, then set it down, leaving a ring on her wood table.

"Is that a compliment, backhanded or otherwise?" Emilia forced herself not to wipe away the wet spot.

"Just a statement. God, you women. Got to come armed and ready with a compliment, or else anything you say gets taken as an insult."

Saul had always possessed the ability to sneak under Emilia's defenses with his barbed comments, yet he always claimed that his comments were not intended to wound. A conversation with him, she thought, was an exercise in psychological warfare.

Saul shook a cigarette out of its pack and lit it, without so much as glancing around for an ashtray. Emilia rose to fetch one from the top shelf of her kitchen cabinet.

"Here," she said, sitting down again. "So tell me what's going on with you. Do you feel like talking about Cecile?"

Saul took a deep drag on his cigarette, coughed into his fist, and gazed up at the ceiling. "She was cold, Emilia, that was all. She was cold. I used to think that the worst part of being in a relationship was having to constantly deal with someone else's expectations. I was always the one who said, 'Listen, I don't talk about love much, I just feel it.' But with Cecile, she was like a glass of water. I kept expecting her to develop some flavor, some intensity about something."

"A glass of water—how refreshing."

"Yeah, and how healthy, and how pure, and how boring. Cecile never worried about my being faithful or our age difference or my former lovers. All she would do was shrug that damn annoying French shrug and say, 'Let's just see how it happens.' Talk about self-possessed. Everything with her was so neat and tidy. I always felt like farting, just to see her react."

"What attracts us repels us," said Emilia.

"Your turn to talk. You been fucking women these days?"

"Wouldn't that titillate you. Why is it that men love the idea of women in bed with women?"

Saul cracked his neck, craning his chin to the left, then to the right. "Sorry," he said with a grin, unrepentant. "But you asked me about my love life."

"You presented me with it."

"Same old Emilia. I've had cats that were more careless where they put their feet."

Emilia nodded her head in acquiescence; the comment pleased her. She had worried that her guard was not up high enough to protect her recently fomented emotions. "So," she said, "does this mean the marriage is over?"

"Yeah, well, I guess that's the way of it."

There was a long pause between them, a wordless collage of impressions which included the rug, Saul's dirty white socks, the oil painting of a red slash in an orange swath, a faint smell of boiled chicken wafting through the open window, the hum of pipes from behind the wall, a wool-inspired itch in the middle of Emilia's back, and a distracting shout from the street. Had she really feared this meeting, Emilia wondered, cut her hair for him, agonized over her choice of clothes? She felt relieved by the lack of tension. They seemed to float together in a warm bath of silence, she and Saul, without the tenderness which would have made their mute accord a small concession to intimacy. Her unfed appetite seemed to have extinguished itself.

Then Saul invoked the power of the past. "Emilia. Do you remember the first place we made love?"

For a moment she could not remember making love to him at all, except in the abstract. Then she glanced at his face, and his knowing smile brought it all back: the passionate clenching of his hands on her hips, the rattle of the stove as their legs bumped against it, and Saul, that other Saul of years ago, moving inside her with such tenderness that she thought her body was being sewn into her soul, stitch by stitch, until there was no knowing where sensation ended and emotion began.

"Which first time?" she replied after a while. "We've had so many."

"Ah," Saul said appreciatively. There was a pulse of something indefinable between the two old lovers, as if they had just heard the strains of a forgotten favorite song on a car radio, and were breathlessly waiting for the car to drive away.

Neither of them moved toward the other.

"I'm a bit put off by this," Saul said. "I didn't expect it."

"Expect what?"

"To enjoy myself. Although the truth is, it's not really fun having fun with you anymore. In fact, it's mildly painful. Do you know, I find myself wanting to touch you right now."

"Resist the urge. We can do without the complications." But what a delight to be so wanted! Emilia could feel the sheer joy of it down to her toes.

"Of course." Saul's smile was wicked. "So how about a hug, then?"

"A hug I can manage."

"So come here, Emilia." He patted the couch beside him.

"You come here."

Deliberately, responding not to words but to intent, not to text but to subtext, Saul took off his shirt, and Emilia, flinching, thought about the layer of fat around her waist.

"Don't be ashamed with me, Emilia. Not with me."

"I'm getting heavy again."

"Show me."

Saul kissed the fold of her breast where it escaped from the side of her brassiere, then the full warm spill of flesh which burgeoned above. "Beautiful," he said, looking into her eyes.

"We're going to make love, aren't we?" Emilia's voice held despair. Back again! It hadn't been such a distance after all.

Those arms had once been home to her; the imprint of her presence lingered still. Twenty-two years old again, insecure again, in his thrall again.

"Only if we want to. Do you want to?"

She said yes, and he took her with passion, all the way back to square one.

ROMANTIC ILLUSIONS

~

Saul made love to his Emilia with the surest of touches, the gentlest of looks, the firmest of thrusts, and the most abandoned of embraces. He left her sighing, resplendent in her nakedness, asprawl on the carpet Vanessa had so admired. Time outside of time, they made room for each other in their separate lives, opening and yielding, until, with a sentence, Saul shattered the truce.

"I wish," he said, "it was you carrying my child, instead of Cecile."

Emilia sat bolt upright. "What?" She knew better than to be stunned at Saul; instead, she was stunned at herself. Where in her mind had she misplaced this information, that Cecile was carrying Saul's child? Had she assumed a canceled wedding meant a canceled pregnancy? She had. In some small white room in her subconscious, she had performed the necessary mental operation and blotted the fetus out of existence.

"She's having it?" Emilia asked, to be sure.

"She said she still wants to. She wants to raise the kid in

France, though, and she said I don't have to feel responsible. It's her decision, she said, and she's taking full responsibility."

Dumbfounded, Emilia pulled away from Saul. "And you don't mind? You have no plans to see your child come into the world? No plans to support it?"

Saul grabbed his pants, dragged them down from the couch, and shook his pack of cigarettes out of the back pocket. "I'm interested, sure," he said, talking around the cigarette as he lit it, "and I'll try to get over there once a year or something. We haven't talked about it yet. But as for finances, supporting a kid that's around is one thing, and supporting a kid that's not even in the same country with you is another." Saul exhaled. "And that's not how she wants it, anyhow."

"That's true, and yet ..." Emilia tried to collect her thoughts. "I've always felt that whatever happened, you and I would always return to each other. Now someone else has a claim on you. There's some part of you and Cecile that's bound together forever now."

"What are you saying?" Saul's voice was dangerously soft.

"I suppose I'm saying that with Cecile, you tried to make a break with us and the past, and you succeeded. I can't just go back. It's over, Saul. This time we're really through." Emilia said this with quiet conviction, as if she really believed it.

"No. Don't say that. Look, I made a mistake—God knows our past together is full of the mistakes we've made—and look at us. We can get back together. We *are* back together." Saul put his hand on her stomach, staking his claim, caressing.

"No, Saul." Emilia sat up and saw the madness descend in Saul's eyes. His fist thumped down on the ground beside her, meant not to hit but to intimidate.

"Why are you doing this to us? Why? Why? Every time I

have a hope!" Thump. "Every time I see a way for us!" Thump. "You keep fucking me over! What is it with you! What is it?"

"Look at yourself, Saul. Look at what you're doing right now. Is this me? Is this my doing?" But it *was* her doing, she realized. She was ending their affair.

"You bitch," said Saul, "you bitch. You're only punishing me because I've dared to do what you haven't—create something original, create life. You're jealous, that's what you are, jealous and dried up and barren of feeling. Your work is shit, it's just another outlet for your man-hating conniving spirit, just another instinctive Oedipal reflex, all fucking fallout from your lousy fucking relationship with your father."

Emilia began to cry.

"Ms. Feminist. Bullshit! You're not even fooling yourself! God knows how your students put up with you. I mean, what do you read in your spare time?" Jumping up with surprising agility, Saul strode over to the bookcase where Emilia hid her romance novels behind the *Oxford English Dictionary*. "Here! Here! Here!" he said, throwing them at her, hitting her in the head with *Love's Passionate Fury*, bruising her arm with *Wild, Free Abandon*, slamming her in the breasts with *A Promise of Forever*.

"This is who you really are—a dried-up old spinster daydreaming romances with the help of high school dropout authors and a quick right hand! That's you, my darling, a pseudointellectual who really wants a strong man to lead her into everlasting love and conventional bliss. But if you ever found him, oh, if you ever found him"—Saul made a crude gesture with his hand, covering his crotch—"you'd cut his fucking balls off, wouldn't you, just to deny yourself, just to keep from facing what you really are!"

Emilia lay huddled and sobbing on the floor as Saul put his clothes on. But when he reached for the doorknob, something broke inside her and she began clutching at his legs, pleading with him not to leave. At first his cold hands tried to peel her fingers off, but as she continued to beg, to repent, to kiss his thigh, she felt him crumple. He gazed searchingly into her eyes, and then his knees folded and he knelt down beside her on the floor, drawing her head reverently against his chest.

"Oh, Emilia," he said, "why do we do this to each other? Why must we always hurt each other so, when what we really want is love?" His fingers on her hair were a benediction, a taste of heaven after hell. Struck down, brought up: this was their interminable dance. She looked into his eyes and saw the face of her own despair. She had lured him into this, either craving the intensity of their love or fighting it; she no longer knew whether it was one or both or neither. To sleep with him was to enter the inferno; now Emilia had no choice but to take the entire tour of torment and punishment. Or did she?

"I can't go on like this," she said, unwilling to accept the reprieve. "This is the end of the line for me."

Unexpectedly, Saul simply bent his head in acceptance. Emilia wished he would rant at her again; that way, she would know it was real. And yet there was something more real about Saul's absence of fury than there had been in all his former rage. Emilia shook her head, confused. Perhaps their fighting had been, all along, a way of making what was unreal seem real. If it made that much noise, took that much energy and effort, caused that much pain and grieving, and then created such sweetness and passion after, it had to be love.

"I'm sorry," she said, for lack of anything better. Oh, for something conclusive to say, for something profound, something final.

"I guess I'd better go now," he said. He did not move for a moment; then, sighing, he got to his feet. She saw him out the door, almost politely.

"We both need time to think, Em. I'll—I'll call you." Saul brushed a kiss against her forehead, Emilia shielded herself behind the door, and then he was gone.

He was gone.

THE PLOT DOES NOT THICKEN

~~

In every story there is a certain point at which events, dropped into the pot one by one, come to a boil. Until that point, each event has cooled the broth a bit; now everything bubbles up into action. Or at least this is what *should* happen, but as every cook knows, sometimes sauces do not thicken as they ought to do, and no sauce, not even hollandaise, is trickier to manage than a relationship. When a relationship congeals into a bunch of nasty thick lumps, it takes more than milk and a few whisks to get it flowing again. Or, should you decide to throw the noxious mess out, a relationship cannot be replaced with something quickly purchased at the corner store.

So, for a while, nothing much happened in the lives of Emilia, Saul, Manya, Boris, Arthur, and Ophelia.

Emilia, who had severed one narrative thread tying her to the story of her life, felt herself to be dangling over a fast-running river. She cooked a lot of rich French dinners for herself, read a lot of romance novels, taught classes, and did her best to avoid working on her book or thinking about Saul.

Saul, who was house-sitting for a friend, did his best to live without income. He also tried, without any initial success, to sell an article titled "Women: An Alien Species?" to various men's magazines.

Manya returned to work at Zaftigue, and she and Boris resumed the appearance of friendship. This time it was Manya who teased and insinuated, and Boris who fended off her advances, feeling both flattered and threatened.

In all his years of doing the ambivalence tango, that most popular of mating dances, Boris had always been the one who requested, the one who led, and the one who tired first. To his surprise, he found that the position of passive partner had much to recommend it; it required less effort, it boosted his spirits, and lastly but most importantly, it absolved him of responsibility. Now it was the woman's turn to worry about stepping on his toes, moving too fast, wearing him out. There was only one real drawback. Being pursued, Boris discovered, left him little energy for pursuing. He had never felt less ardent, not only with Manya, but with all the women he met.

Manya, on the other hand, found the role of seductress easier with each repetition. Of course, when she and Boris parted, she felt anxious and drained, but she had often felt that way before she undertook the dominant role. It took no great courage to be bold, she discovered; it was simply a matter of forcing out all weakness for whatever time she was onstage.

As for Ophelia, she avoided Arthur and spent her days painting glowing orbs inside of pyramids on the walls of her room while Arthur brooded and pined for her.

THE WINTER OF
ARTHUR'S DISCONTENT
~~

By mid-December, Arthur had not made love to Ophelia for an entire month. The reason was that Ophelia was in the grip of an identity crisis, and she preferred to vacillate between personae in the privacy of her own body.

This period of abstinence had created a huge rift in Arthur and Ophelia's relationship, as previously all their conversations, their deep conversations, had been physical. Through the medium of sex, they had expressed many things: ambivalence about intimacy (no face-to-face kissing); the desire to be seen clearly, faults and all, and still accepted (complete exploration in broad daylight); interdependency (bondage); the need to be in control (wrestling and ravishment); and sometimes simple tenderness (you must know how simple tenderness is expressed).

At first Arthur had endeavored to retake his lady fair by cajolement and flattery. Then he had attempted more forcible forms of persuasion. Finally, out of desperation, Arthur tried talking to her.

"Why don't you want to have sex anymore?"

"I just don't feel like it right now."

"You never seem to feel like it."

"So leave me alone until I do."

"When are you going to feel like it again?"

"When I do." Ophelia shrugged out of his embrace.

"Is it because you're pregnant?"

"That's none of your business, Arthur."

"What do you mean, none of my business? I'm responsible, in case you've forgotten the mechanics involved."

"You might be responsible. Actually, there are a few contenders for that position."

"You're lying, my sweet, through your sharp little teeth."

"Of course I'm lying. I lie, and have lied, and have laid, and have been laid. But not only to you or with you, so there you are," said Ophelia.

"Conjugating the conjugal? May I conjoin?"

"Feel free."

"Well, my turtledove, you may conceive otherwise, but my conception is that the baby's mine. Now, let's stop this wordplaying around. Why are you doing this? You're acting like we're strangers."

"We were never all that close, you know."

"Are you trying to tell me that we've broken up?"

"Yes. No. Look," Ophelia said, clutching her stomach, "I'm not trying to tell you anything. Let's just leave it at that, okay?"

"Leave it at what? Leave it at we've broken up? Or not? Leave it at you're pregnant with my child and I hav'n't got the faintest idea what's going on?" Arthur could not bear the sight of Ophelia's pale, closed face. He began to shake her. "Leave it how? Talk to me, for god's sake! Leave us where?"

"Arthur," Ophelia said, "quit manhandling me."

"I'm sorry." He released her.

"Anyhow," she said, fighting down the nausea which had been building steadily since Arthur started shouting, "you don't need to worry about the kid anymore. I had it done."

Arthur stared at her. "You did what? When?"

"I took care of it, all right?" She was too tired to elaborate.

"Why didn't you tell me?" His voice rose in what was very nearly a wail. Until this moment he had not realized how much he cared. It was not necessarily that he had wanted her to keep the issue of their loins; it was the fact that said issue's existence had bound them together, had reassured him when he felt that she was receding farther and farther away from him with every day that passed.

Ophelia, unable to bear the look in his eyes, opened a drawer and began sorting papers. There was a humming in the room, the static from someone's stereo next door. "Oh, Arthur," she said in exasperation, "stop standing there breathing and just get out now."

That was when he punched her.

A DAMSEL IN DISTRESS

~

Emilia walked into her class the next day at such low ebb that she had to push at her last reserves just to bring forth language.

"God's wounds," said Ophelia to Manya, "she looks awful."

"I like her haircut, though."

"You must be joking. She looks like she's about to take holy orders, and she's gained weight," said Ophelia, who was beautiful and clear-eyed that morning, with a fine sharp point to her breasts, each like the well-honed tip of a knife.

"She does look a bit matronly. When did she start wearing flat shoes?"

Only Emilia's lips were unchanged, still as crimson as the blood of a fairy tale queen. She looked out at the class: the neo-hippie in her Indian print dress, her heavy wrists supporting fifty beaded bracelets; Ms. Kornbluth, the budding English professor who had searched for *Flesh of Frailty*; the acned biology major in the corner and the pink-cheeked blonde with the perfectly manicured nails; Manya and Ophelia sitting side by side like an improbable pair of cat and dog companions.

Ms. Feminist. Bullshit! You're not even fooling yourself! God knows how your students put up with you. I mean, what do you read in your spare time?

Emilia felt the stab of Saul in the small of her back and wondered what she could say to these young women. She cleared her throat, glanced at her notes, and read off the first line: "When we look at *Mysteries of Udolpho* we see the great-grandmother of the contemporary gothic novel. Femininity afflicted, femininity embattled—but femininity will be saved, of course, by marriage triumphant."

This is who you really are—a dried-up old spinster daydreaming romances with the help of high school dropout authors and a quick right hand!

Suddenly Emilia found herself saying something quite unplanned. "The contemporary gothic novel. Yes. How many of you," she asked, "have read a gothic romance? By romance, of course, I do not mean the chivalric tales of medieval romance, or the romance as a prose piece that differs from the realistic mode, nor do I refer to a text in which the story is overlaid with disquisitions and digressions, as the *Oxford English Dictionary* would have it, but romance as a genre in which a tale of passion, or more correctly, of matrimonial pursuit and attainment, takes place within certain set parameters."

No one understood what she had said, and therefore no one replied.

That's you, my darling, a pseudointellectual who really wants a strong man to lead her into everlasting love and conventional bliss.

"O-kay. Let's try it this way, kids. How many of you have read a goddamn bodice ripper? Let's see some hands! Oh, come on," she said, noting her students' amused smiles, "let's be honest. None of you has read one?"

"I did once," said the well-manicured student, "for a research paper. It was a Harlequin."

"You would choose one without sex," snapped Emilia. "And what about the rest of you? Never read one for fun? Never gotten lost in a nonfeminist fantasy of a man as strong as he is honorable, a man of warriorlike proportions"—someone snickered in the back row, but Emilia ignored this—"a man like a banked flame, burning only for his true love, just as he is tender only to her, showing her his softness as he imparts to her his strength? What, none of you? What is the point of my lecturing about the impact of Victorian images of male and female roles if not one of you feels brave enough to come forward and say, 'Yes, I have had those thoughts.'"

"Maybe none of us has," said the neo-hippie. "You might be better off trying the general college."

There was laughter, the polite academic laughter Emilia

should have been generating in the course of her lecture. Stunned, Emilia lost the surge of adrenaline she had been riding like a surfer on a wave, and felt diminished, inferior, exposed before these supple children. Oh, to be able to fall into a swoon and be absolved of all responsibility!

It was then, as Emilia faltered, that Manya saw the resemblance. Plump, unsure of herself, awkward in her earnestness, bookish—here was Manya's kindred spirit, unveiled at last! But she was defenseless and under attack. Something heroic in Manya's nature rose to the fore, and she gripped her verbal sword in hand and charged into the fray.

"Actually, I've read a few," said Manya matter-of-factly. "Men are always asking if I masturbate to them, but I explain that it's the sheer experience of arousal the books generate that's so pleasurable. Men are all so orgasm-oriented, as the French have pointed out, and this simply *permeates* their experience—not to mention expression—of literature. Is that what you were driving at, Professor Larsdatter?"

"This is ridiculous," said the formidable Ms. Kornbluth, aiming her remark at Manya, but clearly implicating Emilia as well. "I didn't take this class to analyze literature on the level of some night course for secretaries. I'd like to hear some more current theories," she added, as if criticizing the choice on a menu.

There were murmurs of assent as the enemy closed in. "In fact, I have a complaint about the reading list!" "I feel that we're losing a sense of direction in this course!" "When do we get our papers back, anyhow?"

It was then that Emilia fainted, folding like a prayer book until she creased in the middle and fell, none too gently, to the floor.

A LADY IN WAITING

~

As Emilia did not appear to be shuffling off her mortal coil, she was told to wait. It was not clear to Emilia that she would have received immediate treatment even if she had been in imminent danger of expiring; after four hours in the emergency room at St. Luke's, she had arrived at the conclusion that the staff there had a very unusual definition of what an emergency was and what action it warranted. The walking wounded were ushered in to see a doctor, but seldom with haste, and whole families crowded in to wait while one of their number bled or suppurated, clutched limbs or eyes punctured or inflamed.

"Are you holding up all right?" Manya asked.

"I'm fine, really I am," Emilia replied. "You don't have to stay. You shouldn't even have come."

"But I wanted to come," said Manya. She wanted to say more, but could not think of a way to express what she was feeling. Emilia's fall from grace had lifted Manya in some indefinable way; it had been Manya who took charge in the confused moments following her faint. Manya had discovered earlier that she did not need courage to be bold on her own behalf. Now she had learned that she could be bold on someone else's behalf, and that, she thought, did take courage.

Emilia would really have preferred to be alone, but there was such naked hunger on Manya's face, hunger for acceptance and hunger to be needed, that she grasped Manya's hand and squeezed it tightly. "I do thank you. To tell you the truth, I didn't think you belonged in the class at first. I suppose I thought you needed more preparatory work in critical theory. But you're a very intelligent young woman, and I'm sure you'll go far. " Her speech over, Emilia released Manya's hand and sighed. "I have a feeling that we could wait here until we're both feeble with age. Perhaps we should call it a day."

Deflated by Emilia's professorial appraisal, Manya said nothing.

In the far corner of the room, a woman so thin she seemed stenciled into her spandex was abusing the world in a strident voice. Beside her, an old man with a genial smile and mottled skin who had been trying to sleep on a chair voiced a mild complaint. The security guard walked over to them.

"I'm sorry, but you'll have to leave," the guard said. At first Manya thought he meant the woman, but then saw that he was speaking to the old man. "There's no sleeping in here."

"But I'm shick."

"Come on, buddy, time to move on."

"Jus' shake my hand," said the old man, "so's I know we friends."

"I don't touch nobody," said the guard, a burly six-footer. "Not safe to touch nobody these days."

"Fucking faggots!" screamed the thin woman.

"Shut the fuck up!" shouted a very pregnant teenager.

Emilia looked at the girl and had a fleeting thought about how the young were never convinced that sex and conception were connected until the proof was in the pudding. She, on the other hand, had never played the game of pretending to be so overwhelmed by passion that she threw contraceptives, like caution, to the wind.

I wish it was you carrying my child, instead of Cecile.

Oops. Emilia replayed the scene with Saul in her mind. Had

she edited out the banal detail of getting up, going to the bathroom, inserting the diaphragm?

"What's wrong? Professor Larsdatter? Are you all right?"

Emilia swallowed hard. "I just want to look at something," she said, rummaging around in her briefcase for her Filofax. Finding it, she consulted her calendar. Was it possible?

"Miss Larsdatter?" The woman at the reception desk, her hair wound in tight little curls by the styling wand she kept in her purse, said that they were ready for her inside, room C.

"That's me." Emilia stood up, and Manya silently handed her the briefcase.

"Do you want me to wait for you?"

"I'd much rather you didn't."

Manya watched Emilia as she walked away; unconsciously, she still moved as if she were wearing high heels, with a slight swagger of the hips.

Room C turned out to be yet another way station; half an hour passed before Emilia saw a doctor.

"Hello," he said, "I'm Dr. Farrell." His grin revealed small, crooked teeth, too many, it seemed, for his mouth to hold. His hair was sandy and fell with unfashionable thickness over a narrow skull. Emilia related her symptoms and her suspicions and then followed him into the examining room. His hands, long-fingered and cool, were gentle as they prodded, and his expression remained one of polite and forthright good nature. Even the steady laconic banter he kept up as he examined her seemed an added courtesy, a verbal towel draped over her for modesty's sake.

"So I went back to medical school," he was saying, "and here I am, an intern, at my age!"

"That's funny," said Emilia, flinching as he touched a sensitive spot. "I have a friend whose fiancé—or ex-fiancé, really—went back to medical school too. Perhaps it's a new trend. Were you by any chance an actuary?"

An uneven splotchy flush climbed over Dr. Farrell's prominent Adam's apple and halfway up his fair, gawky farmer's face.

"Are you—your first name is Jack?" Dr. Farrell nodded, and Emilia flinched again. Here she was, falling apart, losing control, and whom should she meet in this charnel house but Serena's Jack, a Jack who, it turned out, had eyes that tilted wistfully down and then lifted at the corners into a bouquet of lines, a Jack whose light touch imparted a sense of respect, even reverence, for human flesh, a Jack who was an altruist, a Jack as unassuming as he was charming.

"So you're Emilia. How strange. I've wanted to meet you for some time. Serena always said that she had to introduce us because she knew we'd get on together, but—well, it just never happened, I guess." Jack shrugged his shoulders and smiled in embarrassment.

"She probably thought we'd run off together," Emilia said, and instantly regretted it. "It's awkward, isn't it, us meeting like this? I suppose we'll have to get together for a drink someday." Worse and worse; now it sounded as if she were trying to pick him up.

"I'll be back in a moment," said Jack. "I think we might just want to do a blood test and see whether or not your suspicions are founded."

But Jack did not return, and Emilia received her test results three hours later from a nurse whose enormous right breast bore the name "Hilda."

The diagnosis was as shaming as it was ironic: hysterical

pregnancy. Those were not the words Hilda used; she couched the verdict in vague medical terms and suggested that it was too early to tell. It did not matter. Emilia's subconscious, which had been hatching this plot ever since the breakup with Saul, was revealed to her in its true colors. She had not been willing to let go of Saul after all; her body had contrived this ruse in order to repossess him.

Adding insult to psychosomatic injury, Emilia arrived home to find a message from the dean on her answering machine. From the dean, not his secretary; if the news was not wonderful, Emilia realized with sinking heart, it would be dreadful. And she did not suppose for one instant that the news was going to be wonderful.

A FAREWELL TO OPHELIA

Manya watched Ophelia getting dressed. She still considered herself an understudy, and felt that she learned as much from observing the cool self-possession with which Ophelia applied black kohl to her eyes as from listening to her philosophy of love.

On this Friday night, however, Ophelia had no snippets of wisdom to offer. She seemed unusually preoccupied as she stood in front of the mirror, wearing a thin silk shirt, white, which revealed the angular fullness of her breasts, and minuscule black panties. "Damn," she said as she tried to fasten yet another skirt around her waist. When she bent to remove the offending article, Manya saw that her buttocks were as firm and globular as a very young boy's.

"So," said Manya, "I left after Professor Larsdatter was admitted. What do you think's the matter with her?"

Ophelia checked her makeup in the mirror; she had lined her eyes in the style of the ancient Egyptians. "I haven't the faintest idea," she said, too distracted to notice the pun. She turned, revealing a small surge of belly that might or might not have been an accident of posture. "Maybe she's pregnant."

On the radio, a whining Irishwoman sang about how no one understood the reasons she was cruel to children and animals.

"Do you really think so?"

"Do I really care?" Ophelia pulled off her silk shirt. Keeping her back to Manya with uncharacteristic modesty, she donned an old terrycloth robe. "Listen, do you have anything I could borrow?"

"What, clothing? You must be crazy. Everything I have would be huge on you."

"I feel like wearing something baggy. Do you have a suitable shirt?"

"I guess. Where are you going?" Manya asked.

"Friend of a friend's party. I'd invite you along, but they're a wild crowd."

Manya, who did not have the energy for a party, nevertheless felt affronted. "I would have thought that after all your tutoring, I was past the stage of being a social liability."

"You have made progress, but this is no party for beginners. You know Gregor—tall, models in the nude for those jeans ads, put on a play about genital scraping of civets for perfumes, completely ambisexual? Well, he's the host. His crew would chew you up and spit you out, and I'm in no mood to mother you through the experience."

"Is Arthur going?" Manya could not keep the petulance from her voice.

"I haven't the foggiest notion." Ophelia stroked gel into her hair, slicking it back.

"Did you guys argue? What happened?"

"I guess you could say we've broken up."

Manya, who had been sitting with her chin on her knees, lifted her head like a startled dog. "You have? Why?"

Ophelia rummaged through a box of earrings, plucking out a small plastic baby with a noose around its neck. "He started whining at me about needing to get a leg over. I told him I wasn't feeling up to it."

"Yes," said Manya, "so?"

"So he keeps at me, saying we never talk, we never fuck, what's going on. I say nothing's going on. He says he feels we're breaking up and I'm just not telling him." Ophelia inserted the earring into her ear.

"And?"

"I told him to get out. And then he hit me."

Manya stood up. "He did what? He hit you? Arthur? Where?"

"Here." Ophelia rolled up her sleeve to show Manya the place on her upper arm. A faint purple bruise mottled the skin; it had the rough shape of a flower. "To be honest, it upset him more than it did me."

"I can't believe Arthur would do that. And all you did was ask him to leave?"

"Are you going to lend me that shirt?"

"I can't believe Arthur would just punch you."

"Right. I walked into someone's fist on my way to the bathroom. Oh, excuse me, sir! Was that your hand? I punched myself, just to see how it would feel. My goodness, that does hurt. I always wondered, and now I know." Ophelia opened a drawer and began throwing articles of clothing into a pile.

"I'm sorry, Ophelia. I didn't mean that the way it sounded. I do believe you. I just can't see Arthur hitting you for no good reason. I mean, not that there could ever be a legitimate reason for a man to hit a woman ..."

"Careful, careful! We wouldn't want to be politically incorrect, now, would we? Mustn't speak before we think, lest those nasty real feelings come out into the open. Wicked Ophelia must have done something to Arthur! Arthur would never hit a woman without provocation—especially a pregnant woman. Especially a woman he made pregnant. Oh, the look on your face, Manya. News flash! Suddenly a missing piece falls into place. No, another piece falls out of place. How could Arthur hit the future mother of his child? The answer—I did provoke him. Arthur was getting all sentimental at the thought that his seed had taken root. Feeling better now?"

"I didn't mean ..."

"Wait. Let me spare you the effort. If I'm in trouble, you'll be right there by my side to hold my hand. Only it's not my hand that'll be hurting."

"I will be there for you, if you'll let me," said Manya softly. "I'd like to be able to help, if I can."

"Help yourself to Arthur and his famous traveling erection."

"Ophelia," said Manya, coming forward, putting her arms around her friend. "It's all right."

Ophelia bowed her head. Her shoulders began to shake, then her breasts, until finally she was crying deeply, brokenly—a response Manya had never expected or thought possible to evoke.

"I can't begin to tell you," Ophelia said, raising her eyes to meet Manya's, "how much I fucking hate you. The pair of you! Why don't you leave me alone?"

"I just wanted to help," Manya said, letting her arms drop.

"You," Ophelia spat, "you just want to feel that someone's more screwed up than you. You just want to feel like Florence fucking Nightingale. I know more about helping than you ever could, Manya. I helped you, didn't I? Before you met me, what did you have in your life but fat, food, and fear? I took you in. I shared my plans with you, not to mention my lover, gave you a taste of the world, a bit of confidence. Not that it'll help much; you're a sponge, Manya, a shapeless, porous suck-up sponge. You still want my advice? Here it is. I advise you to give up on that Boris of yours, before you make a complete ass of yourself. So he said he loved you once. 'When the blood burns, how prodigal the soul lends the tongue vows.' And his blood doesn't seem to be burning for you now, at any rate. You really are a joke, Manya. I don't know why I bothered."

"I'll tell you why you bothered," said Manya, biting down on each word as if faster speech would choke her. "It's because you like to have people hanging around you, people who can stare at you in awe and make you feel superior. Arthur and Manya, Ophelia's disciples. A lover who can barely show emotion—but when he does, wham! He's out. A girlfriend who doesn't give you a moment's competition, but you'd rather have her hate you than ask for her help. Are you frightened that if people got too close they might notice that you're as fake as your hair? Oh, and another thing—all those lovely quotes you have. Most people don't have to recite from rote like a parrot, but then, most people have something to say about themselves. Maybe the real reason for this Doomsday Coalition is to give you something to talk about, a conversation piece, a big glossy book that sits on the coffee table and that no one reads. Well, let me tell you something, Ophelia. I understand why Arthur punched you. He was probably trying to get some kind of response out of you that wasn't memorized beforehand."

Ophelia put her hand on her stomach and took a deep breath, and suddenly Manya remembered that she was pregnant. "Ophelia," she began, "I'm sorry, I ..."

"No. It's all right. Thank you. You've made things very clear to me." Manya searched her friend's face, surprised to see something altered in it. She was reminded of horror films where the vampire, mortally wounded by a stake in the heart or by the rays of the rising of the sun, turns anguished mortal eyes to its attacker and says, *You have released me.* She had reverted to human form, had Ophelia, to a form Manya had never seen before. It was Jane Saunders who stood before her now.

LA BELLE DAME SANS MERCI

~

Oh, what can ail you, Arthur unarmed, alone and palely loitering? A crust has formed on the beer bottle pyramid in your room, and no music is playing on your stereo.

"I met a lady in the meads," Arthur muttered to himself,

plucking at the strings of his guitar. "Full beautiful, a faery's child. Her hair was short, her ass was cute, and her eyes were wild."

It was Saturday morning, very early. Arthur had searched for Ophelia all through the night. He had been to Gregor's party, to her favorite trendy bar near Columbia, and to her favorite pub in the Village; he had been to four different fashionable clubs and three greasy spoon restaurants. He had drunk whiskey, Jell-O shots, beer, and black coffee. He had eaten nothing but his heart out.

Now, sitting in Ophelia's empty room, Arthur began searching for clues to why she had disappeared from his life. There were no diaries, no revealing poems or notes, only her artist's pad. Arthur flipped through the pages until he found Ophelia's self-portrait. But what was this new addition scrawled across the lush and fecund flesh? THE ONE MISSING IS THE ONE WHO MADE THIS PICTURE. What did it mean?

Arthur caressed the heavy drawing paper, touching the mocking ink eyes and unsmiling mouth, skimming over the heavy pointed breasts, lingering over the slight distended pout of her belly, stopping where the thick black message intruded across her thighs. Arthur scratched his head in mystification. It could not be a mistake. Ophelia was not impulsively destructive; she plotted her acts with a playwright's care. She would not deface her own work for no reason. This was a test of sorts. He tried reversing the words: PICTURE THIS MADE WHO ONE THE IS MISSING ONE THE. It still made no sense. There must be something he was missing—wait. Shakespeare. If he were to discount the spelling and pronounce "the" with a long 'e' ...

Picture this maid who won thee is missing one—thee.

BORIS IN HELL

~~

Boris fell asleep while watching an old Hollywood musical on television. The last thing he remembered seeing before his eyes shut was a beautiful blonde in a white gown ascending a celestial staircase that spiraled upward through the clouds. The last thing he remembered hearing was the sound of violins reaching a crescendo.

The next thing he knew he was in Hell.

Hell was a place much like Club Med. There was a simple wood shack which served tropical drinks, beer, condoms, and bathing thongs, a sprawling swimming pool in the shape of a lagoon, and a lot of people with reasonably attractive bodies and tense, smiling faces.

"Hi. I'm Lucy. Welcome to the Last Resort," said an attractive woman wearing red eyeglasses and a surprisingly modest one-piece red bathing suit. She looked to be about Boris's age and had the deep-breasted, almond-eyed look Boris associated with women of his ethnic background. Her hair, which was tied back, was thick and brown, and she had a narrow forehead. Despite her warm greeting, there was something stubborn and tired in her expression; she reminded him of someone, vaguely. The resemblance was not so much in the details of her appearance as in the overall impression. She carried a clipboard and a ballpoint pen.

"Name, please."

"Boris Kaminsky."

Lucy found his name on her list and scratched a check next to it. "Great. Okay. This is the outdoor pool; there's a heated one inside the main building. Your cabin is in the K section—hold on, here's the map and brochure—and you can always ask one of the staff for help. Staff wears red, but the seasoned guests will probably be able to answer any of your questions. Oh, yes, one other thing: towels are free. Unlimited fresh towels here." The woman smiled. "Hope you enjoy your stay." She turned and began to walk away.

"Excuse me, umm—Lucy?"

A look of vexation crossed Lucy's face for a fraction of an instant as she returned. "Yes, Boris?"

"Am I really ... is this Hell?" For he knew where he was, as one knows such things in dreams, where the mysterious is obvious and the obvious mysterious.

Lucy gave a little artificial laugh, like a hostess with too many guests. "Yes, it really is. Why, did you think it was Heaven? Don't be embarrassed—lots of people make that mistake at first."

Boris looked around. A handsome young man in a red bathing thong walked up the lifeguard's chair, replacing a handsome young woman in a skimpy red bikini. A male guest hopped awkwardly on the hot cement, having neglected to wear his flip-flops. He gave a loud sigh of relief when he reached the pool, where a blonde in a pink bikini was wading listlessly in the shallow end. Boris turned back to Lucy. Her attire suddenly seemed dignified rather than modest, a badge of rank.

"Lucy, as in Lucifer? You're the Devil?"

Lucy nodded.

"And the staff—demons?" She nodded again, but more impatiently this time. Boris thought for a moment. "It doesn't seem right. People pay to go to places like this. Is Hitler here? Is the blonde in the pool a mass murderer?"

"Before I answer, I must inform you that my time is limited. Three questions per newcomer, that's all I can afford. I'll make an allowance for initial disorientation and count this as your first question. Clearly Hitler and mass murderers don't end up here. Hell has many levels. Now, think carefully. Only two questions more, and then I really must leave you. I have a new arrival on level G, and he's bound to be a handful—he's wearing a T-shirt that reads, 'Kill Them All: Let God Sort Them Out.'"

"You're not at all what I expected the Devil to be like."

"Don't flirt, Boris, you have all eternity for that."

Boris, who had been about to suggest a drink when she was through working, felt a chill enter his blood. "All eternity?"

"Where are you keeping your head, Boris? Did you think this was a vacation? Did you think this was fun and games? This is damnation."

The Devil was beginning to remind him of his mother, and this struck him as amusing. "But this *is* fun and games," he said. "If this is Hell, what's my punishment? Answer me that."

"Answer yourself that, smart boy."

Then, without transition, the scene changed, and Boris saw himself and his mother seated at a small round table with a white tablecloth. A disembodied voice was speaking with the intrusive tone of a narrator in a Victorian novel. It said:

When Boris was nine, his mother took him to a café as a special treat. She told him to order whatever he liked, and Boris looked around with hungry eyes at all the cakes displayed like showgirls in neat rows, and sniffed the rich perfume of chocolate in the air. He was delirious with happiness; in living memory, he could not recall having such power to please himself. He wanted chocolate cake with chocolate filling, and a cup of hot chocolate with a thick dollop of cream.

His mother warned him not to order both; have the cake with cold milk, she said, or the hot chocolate with a sugar cookie. But she had said he could have whatever he liked, and he liked chocolate, which she always rationed out to him a tiny piece at a time, even though they were not poor. She was always doling out pleasures a drop at a time, and there were always huge dutiful bowls of vegetable soup and boiled chicken to be eaten first. A single compliment was given for every thousand criticisms and words of advice, a moment's smile for hours of anxious looks. And this, she told him, was his carefree time; when he was grown to be a man, he would understand that life wasn't all fun and games.

Boris watched as his nine-year-old self ate the first bite of double chocolate cake. Now he will be thirsty, Boris thought, and with that thought, Boris became his nine-year-old self drinking the hot chocolate with cream under his mother's watchful gaze. He gagged at the cloying rich taste of chocolate. Sweat broke out on his forehead, but his mother forced him to finish it all. She nodded her head in satisfaction as he lifted his fork to his mouth more and more slowly; he might as well have been having her soup and boiled chicken.

The voice of the narrator came on again. As if making a pronouncement of great significance, it intoned: Boris never ate chocolate again.

"But that's not true!" Boris protested. "I did eat chocolate again." And then he was back in Hell, and Lucy was checking her watch.

Boris looked the Devil in the eye. "You are evil," he said.

"You expected maybe loving-kindness? Care and concern? Not that love and kindness ever had an effect on you. What did you think, Boris—that life would be an endless holiday, filled with beautiful women and no responsibility? Well, here you are. And don't blame me if you've lost your appetite. I'm only giving you exactly what you wanted."

"If you hadn't always been so stingy, I wouldn't have ordered both the cake and the hot chocolate! It was a mistake, I admit it, but it wasn't my fault. I was only nine, goddammit! How far do you have to go to prove your point?" He was becoming confused, he knew. This was the Devil, not his mother. But the distinction seemed increasingly semantic.

"Listen to me, my son. At some point, a person has got to stop blaming his parents for what they didn't do right. Hell is full of people with bad parents—but so is Heaven. So your father was a *paskudniyak* and your mother was a terrible person. She made you eat chocolate, she lectured you, you suffered something awful. Maybe she had some good points, too. Maybe her heart is breaking because she was the only person at your funeral. If not for her, you'd probably have been eaten by a dog. Well, not exactly a dog, more like a brown puppy with a fat stomach, and what it was doing in a cemetery is anybody's guess—probably digging for a bone. It sat whimpering on your grave as if its heart was breaking, but your mother beat it off with a stick."

That was when Boris woke up, sweating profusely, remembering nothing, surprised to find the sheets knotted around his ankles.

WHAT THE WISE WOMAN SAID

~

That night, as Manya lay on the uncomfortable bed of her thoughts, hearing every random sound magnified, intensely aware of the position of her spine on the mattress and her cheek on the pillow, she found herself tossing from memory to memory, backward and forward in time. She was fourteen years old in a dark bedroom, and Adam Mandrake was trying to fondle her breast as if it were ripe fruit dangling conveniently from a small, still tree; she was in her own bedroom, holding a faunlike stranger deep within the land of her own body; Boris's erection pressed almost incidentally against her thigh, and all her other knowledge of him, a thousand trivial anecdotes of his daylight self, pushed firmly at the barrier of her resistance, demanding entrance.

She remembered food, too; for some reason, baklava, overly sweet and thick with honey, lingered most forcefully. She felt that she was dreaming without sleeping. She did not think about Ophelia. When she tried to recall their argument, she could only focus on the image of Ophelia bending over, her thighs white against the black silk skirt which would no longer fasten around her waist.

Finally, in desperation, Manya got out of bed and took out her old book of fairy tales. Her favorite story had always been the one about three sisters, Little One Eye, Little Two Eyes, and Little Three Eyes. Little Two Eyes was despised by her sisters, and by her mother, who also had one eye. She never had enough to eat, and was fed crumbs from the family table. But one day, when Little Two Eyes went out into the field with her goat, a wise woman appeared to her.

"Why are you crying?" said the wise woman. "Dry your eyes. I will tell you what to do so that you will never be hungry again. All you have to do is say, 'Little goat, bleat, table appear,' and a beautifully spread table will appear before you with the most delicious food on it, and you can eat all you want. When you have had enough, you need only say, 'Little goat, bleat, table away,' and it will vanish."

And Little Two Eyes was happy, until her mother found out and killed the goat. The wise woman appeared again and told Little Two Eyes to ask for the goat's heart and plant it. The heart grew overnight into a tree with silver branches and golden fruit, and none but Little Two Eyes could harvest it; at the touch of a stranger's hand, the branches danced away, just out of reach.

There was more to the story, of course: a handsome knight and marriage and a palace. Manya had never cared much for the ending, and the death of the goat upset her. Her favorite part was in the beginning, before Little Two Eyes's secret was discovered. The picture in the book showed the gold-and-silver tree, but the picture Manya carried around in her head was of a green field and a young girl, seated at a small round table with a white tablecloth, able to eat to her heart's content and then make it all disappear.

EATING THE TENDER HEART

~~

Morning arrived with the brutish punctuality of an unwant-
ed guest. On this cold and windy Saturday, a week less a
day before Doomsday, Manya wished nothing more than to be
old and gray and wise, and not to yearn for male embrace or
male solace, for male ignition or recognition. Manya dressed
as if for a funeral, touched her mourning ring for comfort, and
left for work.

"Pure silk. Now, there's a quality fabric," crooned Mrs.
Blancher. "You can't argue with silk. Of course, I might have
thought I was getting a bit mature for a dress like this, but
your girl here, she knows what she's about."

"Women, like wine, gain their fullest savor with maturity,"
said Boris, ringing up the sale. "Here, for being my best customer." Boris placed a small herbal sachet in the tissue paper
with the dress as he wrapped it up.

"That's what they tell you, you're never too old for anything.
But take it from me, old is no fun. Your bones ache, your eyes
hurt, your joints give you trouble, and every time you read the
obituaries you cross off another name in your address book. Ah,
if only my Hiram were alive—he'd have loved seeing me in this
dress, the old goat. I should have left it for a nice young girl so
it would be appreciated." Mrs. Blancher looked at Boris in a way
that, had she been a less matronly woman, he would have taken
for a leer. Then she shrugged, gave a knowing sort of nod to
Manya, and left the store with her silk dress folded neatly in a
bag and placed on top of her groceries.

Manya put away a red velvet jacket and four dresses which

Mrs. Blancher had tried on and discarded. Boris sat drinking his coffee and staring off into space. A faint shadow of stubble darkened his mouth and chin; he was growing his beard back.

She wondered what he was thinking. She was tired and did not feel well; Mrs. Blancher had been a difficult customer, and Manya had felt an unfamiliar stubbornness settle into her neck and shoulders as the old woman insisted on trying on garment after garment. How could one sleepless night affect her so? Little goat, bleat, table appear. Manya looked up and discovered that Boris was watching her.

"What is it?"

"Nothing." Boris looked away. "You seem different today."

"Do I?" Manya stood, hands clasped and head bent.

"Quieter. Subdued." Boris sipped his coffee. "More like the old you."

Manya slowly unlinked her hands and raised her head. She moved cautiously across the room, as if the floor were unfamiliar territory, and took her coat out of the closet. "Do you prefer that—the old me?"

Boris looked surprised at the question. "I don't know. Yes. I suppose I do." Then he noticed that she was shrugging her arms into her coat. "Are you going out?"

Manya pulled her collar up. Her face was composed. "It hasn't worked out, has it, my being here? It's not what I wanted. It's not what you want. We're just treading water. And neither of us wants to hurt the other. So I think I should go."

"Just like that?"

Manya paused, considering. "I walked in just like that, remember?" She held his eyes briefly, then broke the contact at the precise moment when the extended silence became uncomfortable.

Boris would have liked, in that moment, to do what he felt he was being asked to do: make a passionate avowal of love. There was a silent plea, not in Manya's eyes, but in the movements of her hands as she buttoned her coat, for him to stop her from leaving. But he could not bring himself to act, as he had so many times in the past, speaking words which reflected not what he felt but what he would have himself feel. He had always thought that true love would be of a completely different order from the kinds of love he had felt for other women, as different as silk is from nylon. This confusion of emotions, in which responsibility and kindness were intermingled—could this truly be the richest, softest weave of which sentiment was capable?

They stood facing each other. Manya stretched out her arms, and Boris embraced her. For a long moment, the feel of her body through her coat rendered him speechless with pleasure; never, not even when holding her naked, had he felt more strongly that he loved her.

"I wish I could be better than I am," he said into her collar.

Manya pulled back. There was a faint smile on her lips; she resembled Ophelia. "You're not the only one," she said. And kissed him, authoritatively, on the mouth.

As she sat in the bus riding home, watching the progress of a cockroach that was crawling down the window, Manya thought about fairy tales. Underneath a thin veil of pretty storytelling were the bloody underpinnings of older tales. She had learned that in Professor Larsdatter's class, in a discussion of Victorian mores. Before the Victorians, Little Two Eyes's goat might have been a satyr, a familiar, a sacrifice. The wise woman would have been a witch, or a practitioner of pagan rites. Perhaps the planting of the goat's heart hearkened back to an ancient ritual involving a girl's first menstruation, or the loss of her innocence.

The bus stopped suddenly, shaking the roach loose from the window. Manya could not bring herself to crush it under her shoe.

FREE FALL

~

Emilia stepped into Dean Manderley's office as if she were stepping off an airplane at altitude, with fear and bravery. She sat in her seat holding the arms of the chair as if they were parachute lines while the dean—who had a pleasant face if you discounted the fact that his features were too small for his large, bald head—smiled uncomfortably.

"Well, well, well," said Michael Manderley, rubbing his hands along the back of his neck as if preparing for some athletic feat. "How have things been going, Emilia?"

"Fine," said Emilia. "I've made of a lot of progress with my book, even though it's difficult finishing it with my teaching load. I was planning on plowing through it this summer."

"Time," said Dean Manderley in a ponderous, lecturing tone. "It's the one thing we academics lack more than money."

Emilia laughed weakly. Was he planning to cut her pay? "Too true," she said. "Still, we muddle by, don't we?"

"Sometimes we do. Most times we do." Manderley raised his thin graying brows over his narrow gray eyes. "But there are times, to my deepest regret, Emilia, when we—don't." He gave an eloquent shrug of his shoulders. Then his hand darted under the desk and retrieved a piece of paper.

"What is this?" Emilia took the proffered page and scanned it.

"It's a letter from Alphonsine Guillaume. It's about you."

A sickening lurch in Emilia's stomach brought her lunch back to her throat. Alphonsine Guillaume, the enfant terrible of French literary theory, the woman who had written *Why the Novel on Your Shelf Does Not Exist, Orgasm as Literature, Literature as Orgasm,* and *U and I Are a Sequence of Symbols,* had written Dean Manderley a letter about her? Alphonsine, whose fame in Europe rivaled that of movie stars, who had turned down an offer to have the new bust of Marianne modeled on her lovely face, had heard of Emilia Larsdatter?

If Dean Manderley's expression had been only a little less grim than an executioner's, Emilia would have been jumping up and down for joy. Instead, she gasped for air, held her breath, and read the letter.

... I am compelled to object, therefore, to the article of Professor Larsdatter last January, in which she called the recurrent theme of the mangled foot in Flesh of Frailty an aporia over which any conscious reader must stumble. Certainly, this refers to my own theories on symbol systems in flux, but in a manner which loses totally the central elements of my argumentation. Were the finished product less shabby I would perhaps be more inclined to agree that imitation is the sincerest form of flattery, but in such a case as this I would prefer the insult proper. I understand that in the garment industry there are spies of fashion who come to France to copy the designer gowns and produce, as you call them, "cheap knock-offs," but we in the arena of academic endeavor have another term for such conduct. Accordingly, I suggest that Professor Larsdatter would do better to study modern literary theory than to teach it.

Emilia looked up. "Dean Manderley," she said at last, "I am shocked and dismayed. If I touched upon Guillaume's arguments, it was not to produce a restatement of her theories under my name. I simply disagreed with certain of her interpretations, and wished to discuss alternative methods of analysis."

"I'm sure it's a silly misunderstanding." Dean Manderley smiled and waited.

Emilia took a breath. She had been handed the sword; now, like an ancient Roman, she must use it herself or give it to a guard. "Clearly, this just shows how imperative it is that I finish my book, in which I spell out my interpretations and my departures from Guillaume's position more thoroughly."

"Exactly my thinking. And as you just said yourself, with a full teaching load—I mean, I find the summer is over before I even have a chance to plan next year's schedules, let alone ..."

"Goodness, yes." Emilia laughed. "I had actually been meaning to talk to you about requesting a leave, but with tenure review coming up and all ..."

"There's plenty of time for that in the future," said Dean Manderley, not smiling at all now. "I am sorry, Emilia."

"Whatever for?" asked Emilia, and waved the letter. "Clearly, I am being read in high places."

"Yes. Well. Was there anything else?" Dean Manderley seemed to heave a sigh of relief, then changed it to a cough.

Anything else? She had been judged a producer of cheap knock-offs; she knew what lay ahead. Either she would be handed an academic death sentence, or else she would be exiled to some barren prison island, a community college perhaps, there to languish amidst survey courses of English literature.

"I'll let you know," said Emilia, shaking his hand. And then she stepped out into midair, no longer sure if there was time to yank the cord before she plummeted to earth.

PLAIN JANE
~

Jane Saunders sat in a dim corner and sipped at her whiskey. There were three men in the seedy neighborhood bar: the bartender, who might have been the twin of her drug connection, judging from his ratlike face; a huddled figure in a trenchcoat; and a man with wild red hair graying at the edges and an absent, abstracted manner.

"Come on, sister," said Trenchcoat, slurring, "lemme fogyerbuz."

"Let you what?" asked Jane in a bored voice. She had tied a kerchief over her hair and was wearing oversized prescription glasses—her own prescription. Ophelia would never have donned the chunky lenses, but Jane was grateful to hide behind them.

Trenchcoat put his hand on her breast. "Fogyer. Rippergood."

"Gee," said Jane, a flash of Ophelia surfacing, "somehow I don't think so." She lifted his hand and placed it on the bar. "If you don't mind, I'm kind of busy at the moment, courting oblivion and questioning the purpose of existence."

"If you find out," said a voice from four stools down, "let me know."

The voice, intelligent and amused, belonged to the red-haired man. For some reason, despite the almost impenetrable mordancy of her mood, Jane was relieved to hear it.

"I'll fogyerslut. Fogyer." Trenchcoat grabbed her again, this time forcefully. Jane did not respond immediately, but submitted to the mauling with lowered eyes and quickened breath.

"Hey. Hey, are you enjoying that?" Red-hair approached, and Jane looked up at his middle-aged, dissipated face with surprise. His voice was a resonant baritone; she had expected a younger man. "Girl, speak up. I'm not getting mixed up in this for nothing."

Jane thought for a moment. "No," she said, "I don't suppose I am. I'm on the path to self-destruction, you see, with an eye toward complete self-abnegation. In view of that, I suppose I should be enjoying myself. Do you think that the fact that I find this horribly distasteful, even frightening, means that I am experiencing a surge of animal desire to live, or could it be something more profound? Because in my experience, the brief instinctive pulses of life force don't stay with me very long, and if it's just that, I'd as soon discount it."

"I can't say that from my vantage point I can give you any real advice on the subject," said Red-hair, musingly. "I am, as is apparent from my appearance, a bit long in the tooth, and I find comfort in outmoded theories that would no doubt strike one of your years as quaint."

"Are you religious?" asked Jane plaintively, for Trenchcoat was hurting her now with his long jagged nails.

"Hell, no. I'm an existentialist. I believe that there is no inherent meaning in anything, but I feel that it's incumbent on me to invent meaning periodically so that I can continue living, even though life isn't always particularly enjoyable."

"But why bother if it's not enjoyable?" Jane's voice was rising, on the border of panic and hysteria.

"Well, because sometimes it is, and furthermore—aw, shit, to hell with it." And with that, Saul—for of course it was Saul—hauled off and punched Trenchcoat in the mouth. The bored bartender said and did nothing. Saul turned around, wiping his fist on his shirt. "You okay, girl? Girl?"

Sobbing, Jane Saunders launched herself into his arms and clung to her rescuer with enough force to knock him off balance. It seemed to her that there was something both mad and wise about this stranger, something in him as violent and quixotic as the forces that drove her, but channeled in him, tamed to an uneasy truce. She did not know how she knew, but she felt that he was her soulmate, her destiny.

It's a convenient thing to think that you've found true love and a teacher of the true path all rolled into one when you are dangling off a cliff, half wondering why not jump, half wondering why cling to the side. And as blind lunges go, it wasn't a bad one.

Saul looked at the girl clinging to him and said, "Fuck. You're pregnant, aren't you?"

How could he know she was pregnant? Saul's intelligence was highly intuitive, which meant, according to Emilia, that he could process information that seemed extraneous, fit it into a sequential system, and make a logical extension into the hypothetical. What's more, he could do it fast, without knowing what he was up to. It was what had initially drawn Emilia to him.

Jane nodded. Yes, she was.

He sighed. Saul was one of those people who believe that the universe is a strange and phlegmatic place that will play tricks on you and give you your comeuppance no matter what you do. He did not believe in duty or responsibility or commitment as such. He believed that in the cyclic nature of events, the wheel of fortune would inevitably turn so that you faced your starting point. He also believed in accepting with resigned amusement the hand fate deals you. Which is to say that Saul was an absurdist, which is how he had managed to arrive at the age of forty-five without committing suicide, either intentionally or by accident, and which was why he felt justified in forgetting about Cecile. If the universe intended him to care for a young woman ripening with child, he figured it would throw one his way.

"Won't it be interesting," said Jane Saunders, bestowing upon her aging knight a look of utter adoration, "when we tell the child how first we met."

THE END IS NIGH

~~

It was finals week, a week of brightly lit nights on all the dormitory halls, a week when the Columbia libraries were full and the student-frequented bars eerily empty, a short period of time when caffeine and not alcohol was the beverage of choice on campus. Students temporarily put aside their personal woes and devoted themselves to the taking of tests, and Emilia handed out papers to a sea of anxious faces and was jealous, for their fears would quickly be put to rest one way or another.

Manya barricaded herself in her room with Diet Coke,

chocolate bars, Sugar Pops, and textbooks. She snapped her mind onto automatic pilot and set it on coursework. Sometimes her mind tried to readjust the coordinates of its trajectory, not by turning away from the material she was studying, but by shooting upward into the lofty sphere of implications.

For example, while reading about the deconstructionists, Manya hit on a line which described how, in a male-dominated society, woman is the opposite, the "other" against which man defines himself. In this way, woman is also part of the definition of man; we know what we are by knowing what we are not. But what if the "other" is not so other as we might believe? Manya bit into her candy bar and sat for a moment so lost in thought that she forgot to chew.

Then she made a sound of disgust at her own self-indulgence. *Don't think about it, learn it, or you won't get through finals, my girl.* Manya massaged the back of her neck with one hand and addressed herself to semiotics.

Of course, not every student prepared for exams; some prepared for failure. Others needed no preparation for success. Misha, who was brilliant, had ample time on his hands to arrange for Doomsday. His only problem was Ophelia, who had dropped out of touch. He called Arthur, but Arthur knew nothing; Ophelia had not been back to her room since last Friday.

Across town, on the fifth floor of an ancient building on Avenue A, Jane stirred in Saul's arms. "Doomsday," she whispered in his ear. "It's almost Doomsday."

"Whassat?" asked Saul sleepily, rolling away and pulling the pillow over his head.

She told him. "But I don't really care one way or another now," she said. "I have you."

Saul sat up, wide awake. "Are you out of your mind? Get up, girl! Get on the horn with that politico of yours. You can't let an opportunity like this go by. Tomorrow there'll be press climbing all over campus, and what are you going to do? Stand on the sidelines and watch it all on the boob tube?"

Jane was distraught. "But that was the old me. I don't care about fame or notoriety anymore. All I want is to be here with you and the baby. I've chosen life and mediocrity."

Saul gave her a little shake. "Jesus, girl, don't be such a doormat. You can't expect to just sit around and gestate. There's biology and then there's destiny, and don't confuse the two. Now get a grip on yourself and make that call."

With a burst of temper, quickly subdued, Jane obeyed. But not before she felt a moment's fierce nostalgia for Arthur—and for Ophelia.

MORTAL AWAKENINGS

~

When forty looms on the horizon, the heart beats faster, for it knows that midday has passed its first circuit into evening. Night is nowhere yet near, of course, but the day is now so clearly finite that some people already begin folding up their picnic blankets and heading for home. Others linger over the last of the fried chicken, eating things they've lost appetite for; the wisest decide what they want to do with the remainder of the light, and do not waste time bemoaning the fact that there was no coleslaw, or that it rained.

From the windows of her living room Emilia watched the sun settle atop the trees of Riverside Park, and did not turn on a lamp. She stood so still that she might have been the gnomon of a sundial, showing the passage of time by the angle of shadow she cast. The light had almost completely faded, although one last shaft had settled into a corner of the couch, as if waiting out the end of the term with her. *What shall I do with myself now?*

Of course, modern literary theorists deny that there is such a thing as a self, a permanent and intrinsic subject of consciousness, just as they deny that there is such a thing as an author who creates a work of fiction solely from the raw clay of invention. No God, no author, no self, just a menu of texts and discourses. In that case, why would Alphonsine Guillaume charge Emilia with plagiarism? How could she, when such a charge robbed her theories of meaning in a way that Emilia never could? She might as well declare that God is in his heaven and that books exist in the inspired realms of the author's imagination before they are even written.

All this occurred to Emilia. She thought it a good subject for a paper, even though her days of writing academic papers were clearly over. She was suddenly hungry; sour grapes are known to stimulate the appetite.

THE PRIME OF YOUTH

~~

When twenty looms on the horizon, the heart beats faster, for it knows that morning has passed its first circuit into midday. Afternoon is nowhere yet near, of course, let alone evening, but the day has clearly begun in earnest. If you are planning on going somewhere, it is time to leave the house now; others have already set out.

Manya took a sweater from the jumble of clothing on her bed, folded it, and placed it in the bottom of her suitcase. She was not looking forward to going home. She could hear the joyous whoops of her hallmates, and screams of pleasure from the street below her window. There would be parties tonight, revelry and noise enough to keep her awake and lonely in her room until morning.

Occasions of great moment can be terribly trying when your emotions do not correspond to your expectations. Think that you *should* be happy, and you invoke the powers of sadness. Weddings, birthdays, and graduations are all days when we straddle the fence between past and future, a position as uncomfortable on the spirit as it is on the thighs. Rites of passage depress as many hearts as they gladden. Contemplate the irretrievable loss of a former state of being, and that state of being can suddenly seem quite dear, regardless of whether you enjoyed it or endured it.

Manya would have liked to spend the night with someone; instead, she supposed she would go out and spend the night with food. Now, food is not merely food to most of us, any more than sex is merely sex. Food is variously treated in our culture as celebration, as framework for social interaction, as framework for familial interaction, as a method of neatly traversing the border between business and social interaction, as a gesture of caring or control, as a prelude to courtship, as a religious ritual. In all its many forms, however, food has the most significance when it is partaken of with others.

But not for Manya. For Manya, food had the most significance when consumed in private. It was in private that something as simple as a Twinkie was transformed into something halfway between sin and sacrament. That was the virtue of binging; at first it filled the absence of companionship when companionship was desired, and ultimately it made the absence of companionship itself something to be desired.

WHERE THE FAT WOMEN ARE

~~

Where are the fat women? They are rarely seen at restaurants. They are rarely seen at sidewalk cafés. They tend to take their food back to the safety of their lairs before consuming it. They like to herd together with others, to move in crowds. You can find them at amusement parks, always on line, never on a ride. Sometimes you will see a fat woman striding alone, in tight garments, with a proud lift to her head. Her breasts and hips proclaim themselves with every jaunty shiver and shake. She probably comes from somewhere else, somewhere where fat in women is prized. Men look at her despite themselves.

Where are the fat women? Look carefully. Some carry their fat well hidden: in their hips, their buttocks, their minds. They do not appear to be fat to the casual observer, but they feel their fat, the burdensome weight of it, and shun the beaches, the mirror, the bedroom light. If you're not sure, ask them. They'll tell you: I'm fat.

Where are the fat women? Why, they're at the supermarket, pretending their shopping carts carry provender for a family of ten. Never mind the hour, never mind that it's a desperate shopper indeed who stalks the gleaming white alleys of canned goods at midnight. The fat women come out at night, blooming like orchids in the artificial glare of the fluorescent lights, congregating silently at the Entenmann's stand, picking up those white boxes filled with sponge and crumb and chocolate cakes, filled with soft squishy cookies, filled with calories regressive and sweet. Ask any woman who binges; Entenmann's will no doubt head her shopping list. Surely some market researcher somewhere has discovered the connection.

And that was where Manya was—at the supermarket, at the Entenmann's stand—when she looked up from the sticky buns and saw that the woman standing beside her was her former professor. For a moment Manya thought about skulking away, but she mastered the impulse. "Hi," she said.

"Why, Manya, hello," said Emilia, somewhat self-consciously. Her hair, damp and in disarray, had begun to curl around her face as it did when she was younger, and she was wearing her tortoiseshell glasses. It seemed to her that her vision had gotten worse recently, without her noticing. Emilia was not wearing makeup, not even scarlet lipstick. She had a box of chocolate chip cookies in her hand.

Manya searched for something to say. It was in that

moment, when her eyes roamed from Emilia, that she became aware of the presence of the others, of the fat women huddled here and there over brimming carts.

And then the lights went out. "Closing time!" shouted the manager. The lights flickered back on. The fat women looked up, ashamed, and scurried over to the check-out counters. Too late! They were being turned away.

"But they're melting," said one woman, holding up her frozen mini-pizza pockets.

"I just have a few things," another pleaded.

The check-out girls snapped their gum, unmoved.

Emilia and Manya regarded each other in silence. Then they turned to watch the other women struggling to replace their items, or arguing with the manager, or trying to sway the check-out girls.

"You know," said Manya, "there's something about this one man ordering all these women out that makes me think—oh, I don't know—about the implications of being a woman in a male-dominated society."

Emilia laughed. "I could tell him that he's really afraid of the feminine side of his own personality."

"We could refuse to leave."

"He'd lock us in."

"No, not just us." Manya gestured at the others. "All of us." She raised her voice. "We could all refuse to leave the store until we're checked out."

"Yeah," said a brassy dyed blonde who was arguing with the manager. "How about that, mister?"

"I'll call the police, lady," said the manager, cocking his toupee forward on his brow. "You clear your lardy ass outta here."

"Don't you talk to her like that!" Manya was astonished at herself. If the manager had attacked her, she would have hung her head in shame; since it was another woman, she was filled with righteous indignation.

"Listen, fatty, you clear out too. It'll do ya girls good to go without feeding yer face for a night."

"Look at you talking!" said Manya, pointing at the manager's sturdy paunch.

"Yeah!"

"That's right!"

"Leave her alone, asshole!"

"You might have given us some kind of warning so we had a chance to check out," said Manya. "You can't just kick us out without warning!" As she spoke, Manya realized she was actually glad of this chance for confrontation. She was angry. She felt that she had been angry for ages. Anger had been bubbling up like poison in her bloodstream, and she wanted an excuse to fight and spill blood, spill poison out.

"Ya want warning, go join the coast guard, sister."

"You wouldn't have done this to a store full of men," Emilia interjected. "It must thrill you, this chance to exercise your authority over a group of women. I suppose you believe women are hardly likely to fight for their rights."

The manager put his hands on his hips. "Don't give me that crap. I heard it all before. I got a daughter. You wanna be liberated? Fine. Be liberated somewhere else. But this is my store. You don't got rights here. Except for the right to get right o-u-t out."

"Give us ten minutes to buy what we want and then we'll leave," offered Manya, standing her ground.

"You'll clear outta here now, dumbo-jumbo," snarled the

manager. "And don't nevva come back to my store. None a youse!"

In the clean and sterile setting of the supermarket, a rumbling groan gathered force in the throats of the fat women. It was the sound of the downtrodden being trodden upon one time too many; it was the muted roar of those who had suffered in private discovering a common voice and a public forum.

"What is the fucking problem you have with my *weight*?" yelled Manya. "Is it a crime to be fat? Is it a crime to be anything other than model-pretty here in your store? Where do you think you come off, baldy, calling me fatty?"

"And what did we ask for, anyway," said Emilia, coming up to stand beside Manya, "other than to be given a few moments' notice, a chance to buy what we needed? Looks to me like you're outvoted, chum. There're about twenty of us here."

"Harvey! Sam!" The manager called to the two burly employees standing impassively by the door. "Throw them out."

The men approached to lift Manya and Emilia by the arms, and then Manya threw a box of cake at the manager and he smacked it aside, hitting Manya in the shoulder.

"You hit me," said Manya.

"Get the fuck outta my store before I call the police," said the manager.

"I think not," said Emilia. "I think that we outnumber you, we fatties, we lard asses, we dumbo-jumbos." She turned to the other women. "Are we together?"

"I think you touch that girl, you got a real problem on your hands, man," said a woman in a lilting Jamaican accent.

"Let us buy our groceries!" This from a Puerto Rican

woman who rattled a bag of potato chips menacingly.

"Give us maybe a little respect, if it's not asking too much."

"You really should have given us some notice," said a British woman, thumping a bottle of ketchup on the counter for emphasis. The bottle broke, leaking sauce over her fingers.

"And don't you even think about laying your hands on her again!" shouted the dyed blonde. "I've taken judo!"

The wail of police sirens outside broke the tense silence.

DOOMSDAY
~

A very beautiful, very slim, and very blonde newscaster stood outside the supermarket as the first grayish light of morning broke through the sky.

"I'm standing here on the corner of One Hundred Fifteenth Street near Columbia University," she said, "speaking from the actual site of what the police are terming a hostage situation, as thirty or so women are entrenched in the Fresh-Man Supermarket holding the manager and five employees with broken ketchup bottles. The police arrived shortly after midnight, when what had been a small altercation escalated into violence."

Other news crews were setting up their cameras, and curious onlookers were shouting and waving. A few homeless people were doing a good business insisting on money before they would move out of the way.

"According to one of the women inside who spoke with the

police by telephone, the manager insulted and attacked a Columbia student when she objected to being kicked out of the store without due warning. But the real object of these women, it seems, is to focus attention on the plight of over-weight women in our thin-obsessed culture." The blonde woman cocked her head to one side and listened to the trans-mitter in her ear. "Wait, it seems we have an update." She nodded at the cameras to keep rolling. "It seems that the women have agreed to allow one of our cameras inside, on the condition that—am I hearing this right? On the condition that it be operated by a woman—no, by a fat woman." The news-caster smiled broadly. "Back to you as soon as we have more, Donald," she said, and the cameras clicked off.

Meanwhile, not three blocks away, Misha, Arthur, Saul, and Jane gathered with the college rock group Deficit Spending on the broad white steps in front of Low Library. Atop the seated statue of the Alma Mater, two pigeons argued in dulcet coos.

"Where is everybody?" asked Jane meekly, wearing a shape-less black coat that matched the shining cap of her newly dyed hair.

"There's a huge crowd of cameras and reporters by the supermarket," said Misha. "Maybe they're covering us later. We don't really get started for another hour or so anyhow."

"Have you heard from the various groups involved?" asked Arthur, careful to address his question to Misha. How could a woman write a man a romantic message, disappear, and then reappear a week later completely changed, acting as if her lover were a stranger? He wondered if an alien had taken possession of Ophelia's body; that was the only explanation he could find for her strangely muted manner and for her apparent involvement with some middle-aged slob. When he had first seen her approaching the steps, he nearly ran up to her and embraced her, but then he noticed that she was actually holding the hand of the red-haired man walking beside her. She had introduced Misha and Arthur to Saul in an odd, toneless voice, and had barely spoken since.

Misha consulted his roster. "Students for the Homeless, the Wrong Our Rights Committee, Women Against Pornography, and the Save Our Environment people all said they'd be here. The African Connection Rappers couldn't promise. Obviously the Palestinian contingent will show up at the same time as the Zionists, or vice versa."

"If you ask me," said Saul, standing with his hands in the back pockets of his faded jeans so that his stomach stuck out, "they'll all come when the cameras do."

"You mean, if the cameras do." Jane tried not to glance at Arthur. "Maybe we should head over to the supermarket and see what's going on."

The sight that greeted Jane's eyes was impressive; the entire block was a tangle of news crews, police, fire engines, and stalled delivery trucks. An excited, voluble crowd had gathered; students and professors, tourists and taxi drivers, businesspeople and dog walkers, talking and speculating, eating bagels and drinking coffee.

"It's just like '68," said one professor, chewing vigorously. "Spontaneous revolution!"

A hugely obese woman was telling a reporter that she supported the women inside. "I wish I was in there with 'em," she said. "I'd eat the store out!"

"Wasn't there supposed to be some sort of rally today?" asked a young man carrying a sign that read, END OPPRESSION.

"This is it!" shouted another student. "It's the fat women's revolution!"

"No, it's not," said Jane, beginning to slough off her torpor. "Hold on a moment! Hey!" A policeman told her to be quiet. "This is supposed to be the Doomsday Coalition rally. Let me speak to a reporter!" But just at that moment Manya's voice rang out over a loudspeaker, and everyone fell silent.

"Listen," said Manya, "I'm just announcing that we are releasing the manager and the two male employees, but the three check-out women are remaining of their own free will."

An excited babble ensued, and then the manager, bereft of his toupee and splattered with ketchup, emerged with his two flunkies, their hands tied with rubber cleaning gloves.

"Do you care to make a statement?" asked the blonde newscaster.

"Yeah," said the manager. "Those women is crazy. All I wanted to do was close up, and they attacked me."

"Do you have any idea what provoked this attack?"

"Damned if I know. Hormones, probably." With that, the manager ducked his head and walked away to confer with the police.

"Well, you heard it here, folks. Now we are getting ready to transmit to you from inside the supermarket itself ..."

Jane, Saul, Misha, and Arthur watched incredulously as Manya appeared on the screen of a small television set in the back of a news truck. She was standing beside an Entenmann's display, surrounded by a small group of women, all of them overweight, three of them in red-and-white uniforms with name tags, one of them familiar.

"My God, it's Manya! And there, that's Professor Larsdatter!" said Jane.

"Jesus, it's Emilia!" said Saul.

"How do you know her name?" asked Jane jealously, as Arthur snickered. His Ophelia was returning.

A little over two miles away, Boris was walking to Zaftigue when he felt a tingling start at the back of his neck and spread to his ears. *Something big is happening,* he thought, *and in years to come you'll regret not having seen it.* Could it have been that psychic gene acting up again? Whatever it was, it caused Boris to turn the corner. Standing in front of an electronics shop, he stared at the image of Manya on ten different television sets in the window.

She did not look well; the camera did not flatter her. But as Boris watched her face, savoring the sight of her as if he had not seen her in years, he felt a burning hunger for her ignite in his soul. Standing there, he saw her at last from the distance love requires—the necessary distance that makes clear vision possible because all detail is not divulged. "Do you see that!" he shouted at a passerby. "That's the woman I love! I need to be by her side! Taxi!" Startled, people cut him a wide berth on the sidewalk.

How do these things happen? He who was unready for love, commitment, responsibility, intimacy, now ready to forsake the safety of indecision? How do these things happen? Suddenly, for all change is sudden. All things that blossom do so in an instant; but blossoms also have roots that have been growing an untold age upward through the soil. Boris's roots had been steadily spreading, inching toward the sun so slowly that he had hardly been aware of any movement in himself.

We do not always, or even often, know what is taking place within. It's as though we host small governments inside us that hold secret meetings and plan covert plots, and by the time our regular programming—thoughts of jobs and dinner and lower back pain—is interrupted by a special news bulletin, the armed troops are already positioned and the missiles are pointed. In this manner, all too often, we find out that we have fallen in or out of love, or discover that we no longer want to live in Seattle, or realize that medical school was not the right choice after all. This is why introspection is so important; the psyche has no watchdog other than itself.

"We did not intend to start anything here last night," said Manya, "but in response to the manager's unprovoked attack, we were forced to take a stand. So now we throw off the mantle of anonymity and shame and assert our rights as women of ample proportions. I mean, you can spend your whole life battling your body for control, weighing and measuring every mouthful. But some days it all gets to be too much and you say, I deserve a little slice of heaven here on earth. We're so used to thinking in terms of food that when we first felt the stirrings of rebellion, we mistook them for hunger pangs. But what we are really hungry for is change. The time has come for the fat lady to sing her song—AND BE HEARD!"

"You have to admit she's doing pretty well," Jane/Ophelia grudgingly admitted as the crowd outside the supermarket clapped and cheered. "Still, you'd think she'd have put on a little makeup before appearing on television."

"Shhh," said Arthur, forgetting himself and taking her hand in his.

Manya lifted her tired face to the camera. "These days people pick up causes as if they were fashions and then discard them, and maybe our complaint doesn't sound very important compared to the protests of the sixties. But it's hard to care about the larger issues when you're fixated on your own unruly flesh."

"Did you know about this, Arthur?" asked Ophelia/Jane.

"I don't think Manya knew," he replied, pleased despite himself at the implied intimacy of the question, as if he and Ophelia and Manya had never separated.

Emilia stepped forward. "The majority of women in our culture today begin worrying about their weight as soon as they hit puberty, if not before. And with good reason! In our male-dominated, thin-obsessed society, there isn't much of a place for a fat woman. If a fat woman does make it into the public eye, it's because she's made a career out of poking fun at herself. And it's not just in America, either—in Britain, the Duchess of York was hounded by the press for daring to gain weight when she was pregnant. No woman, no matter her position, is exempt from being judged on the basis of weight, an issue which strikes to the heart of women's rights in general. Traditionally, women's connection with food and the home ..."

There was a rumble of commotion behind Emilia, and she turned and gasped as police wearing gas masks charged into the store through a back entrance. The screen went blank as the camera was knocked aside. "Jesus," said Ophelia/Jane. "I don't believe it. This is incredible!"

"Emilia. My God, Emilia," said Saul. "She'd better be all right."

"Look out, out of the way, I'm a doctor, coming through!" yelled a sandy-haired man in the back of the crowd. It was Jack, sprinting from the emergency room, where he had heard the news over the radio. Manya and Emilia and the other women stumbled from the supermarket, coughing and tearing, while the police ringed them, rifles at the ready.

"Manya!" shouted Boris. "Let me by, you pigs! Let me see her!" Boris shouldered his way to Manya and held her against his chest as the news crews captured the moment on film.

"Boris," said Manya weakly. "What are you doing here?"

"I love you," he replied, not unaware of the drama of the moment. It was an epic, very Russian sort of drama at that, and Boris was filled with passionate, epic, very Russian sorts of emotions.

"Emilia!" shouted Jack and Saul at the same time, and rushed to embrace her, each giving the other a dirty look.

"Do you have a statement for the press?" queried the blonde reporter.

"What kind of statement?" asked Manya, confused.

"Anything you say can be used against you," warned a policeman.

"I feel a little sick from the gas, actually," said Manya, sinking to the ground and putting her head between her legs as Boris helplessly stroked her head.

In another corner, a transformation had taken place. Ophelia had taken charge and was telling a news crew that the protest in the supermarket was a plan masterminded by the Doomsday Coalition.

"The undermining of fat women must end now," said Ophelia. "I speak as a pregnant woman who expects to become fat very shortly."

"Who is in this coalition?" asked the reporter.

"Well, there's Arthur, of course—he's my right hand, a shining example of how liberated from fat prejudice men can be. Arthur, get over here. This man," purred Ophelia, placing her arm through the crook of his, "has stood by me throughout the many months I've been organizing this demonstration."

Arthur, staring at his lover's belly, blurted out the thought uppermost in his mind to a watching audience of thousands. "Ophelia! You didn't have the abortion after all!"

AFTER THE FAT LADY SANG
~

The main consequence of what came to be called the Fat Women's Revolution was a marked change on Madison Avenue, where glamorous advertisements depicting overweight women influenced the fall fashion line. Glossy magazines began featuring increasing numbers of large-size models, and actresses who had cut their hair or had their breasts and lips enlarged in other years began to concentrate on gaining anywhere from ten to twenty pounds. *Time* magazine heralded the return of the "Renaissance ideal" of feminine beauty, and the makers of the Yummy Figure liquid protein diet began to advertise their product as "a nutritious, tasty way to put on pounds, fast! Just drink a delicious Yummy Figure shake after every meal. It has twice the calories of the leading competitor. For the woman who wants a womanly figure—Yummy Figure." Eventually television talk shows featured programs warning teenage girls about the dangers of rapid weight gain.

Arthur and Ophelia reunited. Ophelia was permitted to retake her exams and decided to major in art, as her talent for sketching skeletal women with brooding eyes and obese women, fecund and fertile, was clearly marketable, given the tenor of the times. She and Arthur got married so that they could get off-campus housing together. They are expecting their child any day now, and the tests indicate that he will be a boy, and healthy.

Emilia received numerous offers to write a book based on the events of that fateful night at the Fresh-Man Supermarket, and finally accepted the highest bid. That, combined with her frequent appearances on talk shows, led to her reinstatement at Columbia—with tenure. She and Jack spent six months not rushing into things and finally slept together, and even though Emilia missed the passion of her connection with Saul, she agreed to move in with Jack. They have no plans to marry.

Serena and Vanessa moved to the West Coast, and now co-author best-selling romance novels under the pseudonym Titania Tennyson.

Saul entered a Trappist monastery and has not been heard from since.

Misha and Herman Finder are currently living together in San Francisco.

Nothing about Boris changed externally, except that he grew back his beard; yet something subtle and irrevocable had shifted slightly in his soul, if you believe in souls, or in his psyche, if you believe in psyches. Other people call it "settling down" or "getting older," but Boris himself, when asked, simply says he supposes he is at peace with himself—which doesn't mean that he doesn't like to have the occasional argument with a particularly obstreperous customer.

And as for Manya, the sudden change in women's fashions and the restoration of the Renaissance ideal of feminine beauty were a bit of a shock to her; it seemed that many women were now battling to keep their weight up, which was not what she had intended at all. Sometimes people recognize her in the street, and she is often approached to be interviewed, but the very ordinariness of her appearance and demeanor soon deflects these assaults on her privacy. Despite this, the lingering tension of publicity can still make her binge and throw up.

At times, when she sits with Boris in Zaftigue (which initially did a fine business but then encountered competition as mainstream department stores began carrying fashionable clothes in larger sizes), she reminisces about the past. If she reaches out and opens her blue clothbound food diary to any given date, she can recall from the entries the events of the day. Knishes and rugelach was the binge at Zabar's, the day after she'd lost her virginity; nacho cheese chips and Belgian waffles marked her first meeting with Ophelia and Arthur.

Strange, but it is these memories which matter to her now, not the calories consumed and reversed; she wishes she had kept a diary of feelings rather than foodstuffs. She has not gained any more weight, but neither has she lost any, and the notebook is filled and defunct. She would like to throw it away, but she cannot. It is a relic from another time, and as such, she supposes, it continues to have a purpose—although not the purpose for which it was originally intended.

She no longer remembers what she had for breakfast the day before, unless she thinks about it. Most of the time, she does not.